"Just lie here with me?"

Surprise riddled through him.

Erin's complexion blazed red. "I know it seems weird, but..."

Don't be an idiot, Nate's brain warned. *Do not get in bed with this woman.* "If you're sure."

"I'm not sure of anything. Except that I don't feel like being alone right now." Fumbling and formal, they moved side by side on the bed, her beneath the covers, him on top. For a few agonizing moments, they remained that way.

Erin cleared her throat. "May I...may I put my head on your shoulder? Oh, God. Never mind. This was an idiotic idea."

"Shh." Nate slid his arm beneath her and urged her head onto his shoulder. "It's okay. Friends, right?"

"Right."

He felt her nod, closed his eyes. They might be strangers, and their meeting unconventional, but damned if she didn't feel absolutely perfect in his arms.

Dear Reader,

Finding love is difficult these days, as we all know. And it's no secret that everyone tripping along life's path bears scars, whether physical or emotional. In this story Erin comes with the double whammy: severe physical scarring from the burns she suffered during the infamous prom-night car crash years ago and the emotional wounds that are inevitable after such a trauma.

It takes a special man to see past all that to the woman beneath, an even more special man to help the woman see herself as he sees her—beautiful, whole and perfect.

Nate's that guy for Erin, although it takes her awhile to realize it. I hope you enjoy Erin's journey toward self-discovery, and in the process that you discover the truth about yourself. No matter how battle-scarred we may feel inside, we are all beautiful, whole, perfect, and more than deserving of love.

I'm thrilled to hear from readers. You can contact me through my publisher or my Web site, www.LyndaSandoval.com.

Warmly,

Lynda

DÉJÀ YOU

LYNDA SANDOVAL

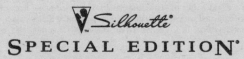

SPECIAL EDITION®

Published by Silhouette Books

America's Publisher of Contemporary Romance

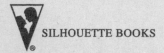

SILHOUETTE BOOKS

ISBN-13: 978-0-373-24866-7
ISBN-10:   0-373-24866-0

DÉJÀ YOU

This edition published by arrangement with Harlequin Books S.A.

® and TM are trademarks of Harlequin Books S.A., used under license. Trademarks indicated with ® are registered in the United States Patent and Trademark Office, the Canadian Trade Marks Office and in other countries.

Visit Silhouette Books at www.eHarlequin.com

Printed in U.S.A.

Books by Lynda Sandoval

LYNDA SANDOVAL

is a former police officer who exchanged the excitement of that career for blissfully isolated days, creating stories she hopes readers will love. Though she's also been a youth mental health worker and runaway crisis counselor, a television extra, a trade-show art salesperson, a European tour guide and a bookkeeper for an exotic bird and reptile company—among other weird jobs—Lynda's favorite career, by far, is writing books. In addition to romance, Lynda writes women's fiction and young adult novels, and in her spare time, she loves to travel, quilt, bid on eBay, hike, read and spend time with her dog. Lynda also works part-time as an emergency fire/medical dispatcher for the fire department. Readers are invited to visit Lynda on the Web at www.LyndaSandoval.com, or to send mail with a SASE for reply to P.O. Box 1018, Conifer, CO 80433-1018.

To Barbie,
Supplier of all things chocolate and caffeinated, and
a damn fine fire captain (and person) to boot.
<SWAK>

Chapter One

The fire raged.

Hot, thick, black smoke billowed and rolled around them inside the four-unit, two up, two down apartment building that was quickly losing its battle with the whipping flames.

Damn unattended candles.

Damn balloon construction on these cheap-ass buildings.

Damn them all if they didn't get control of this thing, and fast.

The fire had ripped through both levels of the apartments almost before the first due units arrived on scene. Numerous engine companies had responded to the first alarm. Engineer Erin DeLuca, her immediate supervisor, Captain C. J. Gooding, and Firefighter Ryan Drake—the crew on Engine Eight—had been assigned to investigate the bottom-floor, north-side apartment. They'd rescued everyone they could find from the entire building; now all the companies concentrated on tackling the fire, determined to knock it down against all odds. The wall of heat stifled her, and she knew it would get worse before it got better. Once they hit the flames with water, the resulting steam would be a hundred times hotter than the fire itself.

Through her helmet's crappy headset, Erin could hear the sounds of breathing, her own and that of every other firefighter trying to extinguish the virulent blaze. Beyond the Darth Vader breathing chorus came the crash of breaking glass; firefighters bumping into walls and furniture in the zero visibility; the *clomp-clomp* of crews moving about in the apartments above; garbled, back-and-forth radio communications as rooms were cleared; and, of course, the snap and hiss of the monster itself. With the cacophony, radio communications were nearly unintelligible inside her mask and helmet. Thankfully, they were all well aware of and accustomed to the limitations.

Her muscles strained as she and her crew carried in the charged one-and-a-half inch hose line that would hopefully black down the fire in this apartment, at least.

"Hillside Command, from Control."

"Go ahead." Erin heard the battalion chief respond to dispatch, from his strategizing position as incident commander outside the fire.

"You're thirty minutes into the incident, sir."

"Copy, thirty minutes. Thanks."

From her spot in the communications center, dispatch supervisor and Erin's friend, Lexy, gave the time. Erin couldn't help the niggling sense of alarm in her chest. Thirty minutes in, the fire was hot enough to melt steel, and it didn't seem as though they were any closer to controlling it than when they'd first arrived. She checked the LED readout for her air tank. Half-full, which meant some of the bigger guys on the scene were likely near empty.

Erin squinted to see through the blackness, but it was no use. She closed her eyes and let her hearing and sense of touch take over instead. She moved to the left, toward the snapping bursts of fire. Without warning, an ominous splitting sound came from above them. Everyone ducked back as the ceiling above them collapsed, raining down furniture and flame, wood and water and the two-firefighter crew that had been in that particular room upstairs. The ash and sparks settled, then everyone moved at once.

Erin immediately dropped to the ground and felt her way to the firefighter closest to her. When she reached him, she leaned down close to his helmet and mask, now jarred away from his face. Bad news.

Fumbling with her stiff gloves, she resituated his safety gear, but not before she recognized him. Her gut clenched. "I've got you, Sully," she yelled, knowing he probably couldn't hear her any better than she could hear anyone else through all the gear. "Can you talk?"

He groaned.

She peered up into the gaping hole just as flames engulfed what was left of the entire apartment overhead.

Her stomach dropped.

"Portable Eight-A to Command, Sullivan's down!" she said into her radio. "Second floor is fully involved. I've got Sullivan and I'm coming out."

"Eight-B to Command, we've got Arroyo," came the voice of Drake, amped to the max. "He's unconscious. Unknown extent of injuries."

"Command, from Engine Eight," came Captain Gooding's calm but urgent voice, "we have a collapse and a fully engulfed second floor. Repeat, we have a ceiling collapse from the second floor to the bottom level with two firefighters down."

From outside, the battalion chief's tone came across with a heightened sense of alarm. "Engine Eight's got a collapse. All units, abandon structure. Repeat, abandon structure."

Three sharp alert blasts rang out over the radio, then Lexy's calm, collected voice. "All units on the Hillside Fire, abandon, abandon, abandon. Repeat, abandon, abandon, abandon structure."

Erin heard the battalion chief calling for a PAR—personnel accountability report—from all the crews working the fire, to make sure no other firefighters were injured or unaccounted for. She hitched her elbows under Sullivan's arms and dragged him first to the wall, and then following the hose line, out toward the front door she couldn't see. Beneath the smoke, she could barely make out Drake and the captain carrying Arroyo the same way.

When she burst into the late-afternoon air, her bunker gear sooty and steaming from the temperature drop, her vision cleared. She glanced up at the apartments, sucking the last vestiges of air from her tank and feeling sick. They probably wouldn't be able to save much of the structure, if any. A total failure.

She hated that.

A Troublesome Gulch paramedic crew ran up to assist her with Sullivan. Erin glanced over, glad to see Brody Austin there, a damned excellent paramedic, not to mention one of her closest friends.

He laid his hand against the reflective letters that spelled out DeLuca on the back of her bunker coat and leaned closer, concern wrinkling his brow. "You okay?" he yelled.

She nodded. Her biceps shook and twitched from the exertion of dragging burly Jeff Sullivan out, and her breaths came in heaving succession, but she'd be fine.

Seemingly satisfied, Brody joined the other medics who had already started administering aid to Sullivan, while Erin ran back to the door to help the rest of her three-person crew deliver Arroyo to them, as well.

She, Drake and Captain Gooding watched until they were sure Sullivan and Arroyo would be okay, then backed off and headed to the designated rehab area. Fans blew cool air around them. Erin sat on the wide back bumper of the ambulance, un-screwed her air pressure regulator from her mask, pulled off her helmet, then yanked her Nomex hood down to dangle around her neck. Finally, she removed her mask.

Relieved to be free of it, she sucked in her first gulp of cool, fresh air. Sweat rolled down her skin beneath her bunker gear, and if her face looked anything like the others', whipped dogs had nothing on the three of them. She stuck one glove under her arm, extracting her hand and inverting the inside liner, then repeated it with the other glove. After she'd removed her air tank and bunker coat, she held out her shaky arm for one of the rehab EMTs to take her blood pressure.

Drake and the captain did the same.

The trio, breathing as though they'd just gone three rounds with the heavyweight champion of the world, watched from afar as fresh teams battled the fire from outside the unstable structure. Once an Abandon order had been given, their only option was to fight the fire defensively.

The head paramedic in the rehab area handed them each a cold bottle of water. Erin downed the entire thing in one extended swallow, and it didn't touch her thirst.

She glanced over at her captain. "We're going to lose this one, aren't we?" she asked, before wiping the back of her hand across her mouth.

Captain Gooding nodded, running fingers through her sweaty hair. "Damn it."

"Will they reassign us, Cap?"

"Probably not. BC called a second alarm. There are enough fresh crews here to take over. Take your time in rehab." She stared somberly at the fire for a moment, then stood and headed over to the other ambulance, where Sullivan and Arroyo were being loaded.

At least they'd gotten everyone out before the fire took the upper hand, Erin thought. Just then, someone yanked her arm from the side. Instinctively, she jerked away, whipping around to come face-to-face with a soot-covered woman who looked to be at least eight months pregnant. Her maternity dress hung in blackened tatters against her body.

"What's wrong?"

"Please," the woman sobbed, barely able to inhale, "help me."

Erin grabbed both of the woman's upper arms, bracing her. "Talk to me! Are you hurt?"

The woman, so hysterical she couldn't form sentences, gestured vaguely toward the building. "M-my husband…"

"What about him?" Erin demanded, giving the woman a small shake. She didn't want to be harsh, but time was of the essence. "Take a deep breath, then tell me."

"H-he went b-back in. F-for the cat." She shook her head and clutched at it as tears streamed down her face. "I haven't seen him s-since. Please!"

Alarm and dread rose inside Erin's throat, threatening to breach her panic dam. She hooked a hand around the woman's arm. "Come on," she said in a kind but firm voice, as she led her toward her immediate supervisor. "Hey, Cap!"

The older woman she respected so much spun to face them, then trotted over and met them halfway. "What's going on?" she asked, her voice hoarse.

Erin glanced down at the frenzied pregnant woman, who looked to be no more than twenty or so. "Her husband went back into the building to look for their cat. He hasn't come out."

Erin's and Captain Gooding's gazes locked, as the captain pressed her lips into a thin line. After a moment, she turned her back, immediately got on her radio and spoke with the battalion chief. They conferred, then Captain Gooding took the woman's other arm gently, supporting her. "Come on, honey. What's your name?"

"Suzette," the young soon-to-be-mother wailed. "We've only been married eight months! Please!"

"Okay, Suzette, okay," the captain soothed.

Between them, Suzette hung her head and gave in to the racking sobs.

"Where are we going?" Erin asked her superior, in a soft voice so as not to be overheard by Suzette.

"Victims assistance," Captain Gooding responded in kind.

Erin gulped. She knew the answer, but hope made her ask anyway. "Are we…going back in for him?"

The Cap met her gaze over Suzette's head, remorse and resignation in her expression. "No."

At the victims assistance staging area, a counselor, and a police officer—Erin's friend, Cagney—sat Suzette down and tried to explain the gravity of the situation. Erin stood back and watched as the confusion and horror moved into Suzette's expression. She knew the exact moment when Suzette realized the truth: her husband was never coming out.

All of a sudden, dizziness assailed Erin. Flashes, images, horrors filled her brain. She couldn't handle this. She started to back away from the cops, counselors and huddled *victims,* hating that word with a passion. She spun, eyes down, trying to block everything from her brain, but her ears buzzed and her hands shook. Part of her boiled with the insane urge to dash into the blazing apartments and search for Suzette's husband, although the chances of him still being alive were zero at this point. Not to mention, her disobedience of the Abandon order would get her ass fired, if not killed.

With no warning, the sky blazed orange as the bottom apartments flashed over, blowing out all the remaining intact windows. Like a freakin' Hollywood movie set. The entire structure succumbed to flames, and thick black smoke blasted out at the fire crews like an angry demon declaring victory.

"Nooooo!"

Erin heard Suzette's keening wail behind her.

Fixated on the fire, Erin struggled to breathe, her knees buckling slightly.

God. She knew.

She knew the pain Suzette was feeling right at that moment. Felt it, all the way down to her soul's core.

For so many years, so many fires, she'd been able to block out the memories of the accident that had destroyed her life, but the unexpected blow of young, pregnant, distraught Suzette had cracked her veneer, and inside lay a mirror. She saw herself in the young woman's eyes as the nightmare of her past rushed in through the cracks.

Prom night. Kevin, the love of her life. Alcohol for all of them except her, because of the secret inside her womb, the baby she and Kevin had accidentally created but had not yet revealed to the world. They were getting married two months later anyway, so what did it matter?

The evening started with laughter and loud music, the rustle of satin and taffeta, bottles passing, sexy Lexy, the prom queen, climbing over the stick shift to kiss and tease Randy.

Then, without warning, screeching tires, a crushing jolt, the disorientation of rolling, tumbling, smashing down the cliff and then fire. So much twisted metal, broken glass and fire.

Screaming, her dress in flames and melting to her skin, Erin saw Kevin crushed and silent. Her best girlfriend, Mick, broken and still. Lexy's boyfriend, Randy, crumpled and twisted inside the smashed cab of the Range Rover, with Lexy trapped and screaming beside him. Brody, holding one of Mick's shoes and walking dazedly around the scene, slipping, falling, getting back up, falling again.

Where were Cagney and her last-minute fill-in date? What was his name again? Erin had thought, as she finally sank to the ground and rolled to extinguish the flames engulfing her dress.

This isn't my life, she remembered thinking. *This is a newspaper article from somewhere else.*

"Kevin!" she'd screamed, clutching her hands to her searing abdomen, as she slowly lost consciousness, remembering, in her last lucid moment, their baby. "Kevin…!"

Erin's knees buckled again, and Brody appeared from nowhere, propping her up by her elbows. "Kevin," she gasped at him.

The lines around his eyes deepened. "Erin, honey. It's Brody. Can you hear me?"

She looked up, disoriented, then remembered where she was and why. She saw an expression of agonized understanding on Brody's face, and sagged against him. "Yes," she wheezed.

"You need oxygen."

"Yes." She needed a hell of a lot more than that, but the oxygen would do for now.

He guided her back to the rehab area, settling her next to Drake and slipping the clear mask over her face.

"You okay, DeLuca?" Drake asked, his eyes wide.

"She's fine," Brody assured the young firefighter, with a confident smile, despite the anguish that showed in his eyes. "A little smoke inhalation. Nothing to worry about." He leaned in, putting his hands on Erin's shoulders. "You listen to me. It'll be okay," he said, in a low voice. "I promise."

"How?"

He looked away, a muscle in his jaw pulsing. "I don't know. But, if I did it, you can find a way."

She shook her head. "We lost someone," she said, her words muffled, breath fogging the oxygen mask.

"I know," he said, his tone somber. "We're transporting the wife. She's gone into preterm labor."

Erin squeezed her eyes shut, absolutely refusing to cry on a fire scene. She'd *never* cried at work. Never.

Brody shook her. "Look at me."

She did.

"We'll help you. Faith and I. It *will* be okay," he enunciated slowly.

She nodded, totally numb, agreeing with him when she didn't agree at all, feeling that nothing in her life would ever be okay again....

Chapter Two

Despite a long shower and half a bottle of shampoo, the smell of smoke still hung in Erin's hair, an acrid reminder of the afternoon's horror. The chief had released the entire battalion after the fire—common practice after such a physically draining event. He'd called in the off-duty shift to cover the rest of their twenty-four hour tour.

Erin didn't feel released, however. She felt as though she'd been holding in a scream for hours, as though she was going to explode if she didn't do something. Finn, her Irish wolfhound, trailed her through the house, whining, toenails clicking on the hardwood. Knowing.

She ignored the ringing phone and listened dully to two concerned messages—one from her mother and the second from her closest friend, Faith—as she dressed in her most comfortable jeans, a well-washed Barenaked Ladies concert T-shirt and some simple clogs.

Clearly, the fire had hit the news.

As much as she loved her mother and her friends, at the moment, she couldn't deal. Brody would fill Faith in, and Mom could wait. Erin couldn't bear to recount the fire over and over and over again. Not now. Not with Kevin's death—not to mention Suzette's husband's—weighing so heavily on her soul.

She'd been in denial for so long, which had worked well enough. Now, this. She couldn't even think about her and Kevin's unborn baby. Sheer panic bubbled up inside her throat.

Go. Just go.

Finn's doggy door was open, his bowls were full and he was used to spending long hours alone, thanks to their twenty-four-hour shifts. Luckily, his abandonment issues had improved greatly. He hadn't eaten a couch cushion or torn up the trash in months. Still, she felt a pang of guilt about leaving him by himself, but she had to. He'd understand. That's what dogs did, what made them so special.

With shaking hands, she swiped her keys and small purse off the countertop and headed blindly for the door, not knowing or caring where she was going.

Her breath came in gasps. Sweat beaded on her forehead and upper lip. God help her, she needed to get out of Troublesome Gulch before her emotions roared even further out of control. Until all those raw, dangerous memories had been corralled back into their neat little mental stalls, gates locked, out of sight and mind where they'd lived for nearly twelve years. She couldn't bear it.

Escape.

Escape.

She whipped wet strands of her choppy-cut hair out of her face, but still it took three tries to get her key into the ignition of her Subaru Outback. By the time she cranked the engine to life, she was so amped that she accidentally kept the key engaged until the pistons squealed in protest. Jamming the stick into Reverse, she spun gravel pulling out of her driveway.

She didn't know she was heading toward I-70. She didn't realize she was crying until she hit the eastbound lanes, and by that time, she couldn't stop. She sobbed until her throat ached and her nose clogged, until her whole face felt swollen with grief. She only remembered to wipe her eyes because she didn't want to risk causing an accident that would force some innocent person to suffer the agony she'd been living through.

Poor Suzette.

She flinched, white-knuckling the steering wheel.

Sure, she had enough of a grip on reality to know she hadn't caused Suzette's husband's death, but she hadn't been able to prevent it, either. Or to help—not even a little bit. She'd lost her damned precious control. Where did that leave her?

It'll be okay, Brody had told her.

Right.

She couldn't be happier for Brody and Faith, or more impressed that Brody had been able to face his demons from that horrible prom night tragedy and come away with the love of the perfect woman. But, some people got lucky in this life, and the rest just muddled through.

Her tears dried up as miles of concrete spun beneath the wheels of her tires, and her face and brain grew numb. By the time the night had darkened to indigo and the pink-and-gold skyline of Denver glittered before her, Erin had resigned herself to a life as one of the muddlers. At least, that's the story she would cling to that night. Anything to keep her mind off…the rest.

She'd survived so far not confronting her issues. Why start now?

She drove until the city swallowed her car, until neon bar signs from a nondescript, yet crowded tavern drew her gaze. Without forethought, she pulled into the parking lot and stopped. Muffled music thumped out from the club's interior. Her vision blurred as she stared at the place, looking without seeing, caring not at all. She jumped and gasped when the tavern doors banged open, and a laughing couple emerged and headed toward a bright yellow convertible.

Talk about adrenaline overload.

After the couple roared off into the darkness, Erin pulled her keys from the ignition and shoved them into her purse. Hands in her pockets, she entered the bar. She made eye contact with no one, because she wasn't there to socialize. The loud music enveloped her into the kind of anonymity she craved. She spied an open bar stool on the far end of the bar near the restrooms sign and headed for it.

No sooner had she sat than the bartender sidled up and lifted his chin. "What's your poison, miss?"

Guilt, she thought. *Horror.* As if she cared. She cleared her throat, but her voice still came out hoarse from the sobbing. "Tequila."

"Shot?"

"Whatever," she said, not meeting his gaze.

Unfazed by her attitude—no doubt the man had

seen it all—he poured her a shot, set it on a napkin with sliced lime and a salt shaker. "Start you a tab?"

She shook her head.

"Seven-fifty."

She dug a ten-dollar bill out of her purse and slid it across the bar. "Keep the change."

The cash register keys blipped, and then the drawer opened. "You need anything, lemme know," the barrel-shaped man said as he pocketed the change, then slammed the drawer shut, its coins jangling like her nerves.

Then, thankfully, she was alone.

With a shaky hand, she reached out for the shot glass. She lifted it tentatively toward her face, but then the smell assaulted her nostrils, and she knew she couldn't drink it. She hadn't been much of a drinker since…and never when she was driving. Certainly not a shot drinker. Tonight, stuffed full with horrible memories, was not the night to violate that particular personal code.

With a sigh, she set the glass back down and rested her forehead in her palms. She couldn't shake the pent-up tension, the racing energy. Something had to give.

"Wanna dance?" came a voice close to her left ear. Wholeheartedly unenthusiastic, she angled her head and eyed the guy standing there. Well, it might at least burn off some steam.

After an apathetic shrug, she slid listlessly from the bar stool and headed toward the crowded dance floor, assuming he'd follow her. She was right.

He caught up and tossed her a grin. "I'm Bill."

She nodded, hooking the long strap of her purse over her shoulder so it rested on the opposite hip.

They started dancing, and the feel of her body moving seemed to mask some of her pent-up emotions. Or at least keep her one step ahead of them. A bandage—not a cure—but she'd take what she could get.

"So…what was your name?"

She regarded Bill, then squeezed her eyes shut for a moment. "No offense, but we both know it doesn't matter. Let's just dance."

Bill shrugged and seemed to accept it.

The more she danced, the more the memories flooded back, no matter how vehemently she tried to fend them off. She needed to find a way back to survival mode. So she danced harder. After Bill, there were other dance partners, but she didn't see any of them, didn't let their names or faces linger in her brain. Who cared? They weren't Kevin, never would *be* Kevin, so none of them mattered.

Her ability to love—to feel, really—had burned to acrid gray ashes long ago. Wasn't that why she lived the way she did, and had, for so long? Alone?

Putting up a façade? Laughing when she wanted to cry? All of it pretty much a lie? What would Kevin think of her now?

The geyser of her emotions continued to erupt, so she danced faster, the multicolored bar lights smearing in her vision. All she knew was, she couldn't stop now, or she'd lose it. Completely.

All Nate Walker had wanted from the evening was a beer or two and some quiet anonymity in which to clear his brain. The night's work had been grueling, the band exorbitantly demanding, as if the pyrotechnic oohs and aahs could make up for their lack of true talent.

But he'd noticed the dark beauty the moment she came in, her hair wild and tangled, eyes haunted. She'd walked right past him without even a flicker of notice, taking a stool at the opposite end of the long, polished concrete bar from where he sat. He'd silently watched as she'd ordered a shot she never drank, and then as she danced with a never-ending series of partners she didn't seem to notice, let alone speak to.

She was somewhere else altogether.

Too bad the guys seemed to view her as right here, right now—and fair game, to boot. His beer had gone warm and untouched as he watched them dance with her, one after another. The more they'd drunk, the closer they danced, and the brighter the predatory gleam in their eyes.

He'd started to curse himself for being here in the first place. He could've stayed in his hotel room, ordered up a meal. Steered clear of trouble until his plane took off for Las Vegas tomorrow. He didn't want to get involved in some dark-eyed beauty's private pain, and yet something drew him to her.

God knew, he'd always been a sucker for troubled women, frail old ladies and little kids who couldn't find their parents. Not to mention homeless mutts. But he'd had his fill of the savior role. It always seemed to backfire.

And yet...

If bad luck hadn't brought him to this spot, on this night, what would've happened to this woman? His chest clenched. For all he knew, he could be the single twist of fate that stood between her and some heinous crime.

It's that kind of thinking that gets you in trouble.

Total melodrama. He smirked to himself. He should write screenplays.

She looked strong enough. Lean and mean—in a sexy, feminine way—but beneath that tough veneer lurked a sweet vulnerability she couldn't quite keep under wraps. It tugged on his heart, and he felt pretty sure that the pack of predators caught on to it, too. His insight, however, brought a wave of concern for her. Protectiveness. The insights of the guys in the bar seemed to be guiding them down a whole different, much more self-serving path.

The waitress stepped into his line of sight.

He tried not to frown. The woman was only doing her job, after all.

"Beer's warm," she told him, pulling his attention from the woman on the dance floor. "Bring you a fresh one?"

"No. That's okay." *Just go*.

"You still want the warm one, then?" she said, leaning her hip toward him in that provocative way that said, (a) she wanted him, or (b) she wanted a big tip.

He threw a ten on her tray, trying not to seem impatient or rude. "No thanks."

She shrugged, set the warm, full beer bottle on her tray, and moved out of his way…just as one of the guys moved in on the woman on the dance floor and tried to slip his hands up the front of her T-shirt.

She smacked his hands away, and swung around into the arms of another guy, who pulled her in toward him and slid his palms down to cup her very shapely rear.

Damn it.

Nate might not want to get involved, but his mother hadn't raised him to stand by and do nothing when a woman was being mistreated. He had sisters, for God's sake. That left him no choice.

With a deep breath of resolution, he stepped off his stool and strode into the fray, glaring away the protests and the men who'd issued them. The woman was already pushing the groper away, so Nate's light tug on her upper arm was enough to spring her loose of the man's clutch.

Placing her behind him, he went nose-to-nose with the man. "Time for you to back off, Romeo," he said, through clenched teeth.

The guy's face reddened with fury. "Screw you. She never said she had a boyfriend."

"You didn't ask."

Standoff.

For a few tense moments, Nate thought he might have to exchange blows with the guy, which he really, *really* didn't want to do. He wasn't a fighter, but he didn't run, either.

Finally, the pissed-off man flapped his hands in a way that said she wasn't worth the fight—which showed how much he knew—then turned on his heel and shouldered his way out of the bar. All the other wolves sank back into the crowded darkness like the cowards they were.

Nate turned toward the woman and studied her face. She really was beautiful, despite her obvious torment. He softened his tone. "You okay?"

She pulled him toward the center of the dance floor and spun around a few times in time to the beat, fanning out her hair. "Just dance. Please."

He started to protest, then decided he'd give her the space she seemed to need for the rest of this song. Maybe she was embarrassed about what had just happened. Who knew? But respecting her wishes was the kindest route.

When the song ended, and another started, she showed no signs of stopping.

Enough.

Nate leaned in. "At least tell me your name."

She opened her eyes, but didn't stop dancing. She seemed to be weighing his question. "Erin," she finally said, in a defeated tone.

"I'm Nate."

She nodded. Kept dancing. "Thank you, Nate. For…that." Her words were almost flippant. Everything about her was incongruous.

He reached out and laid his palm gently on her shoulder. "Erin, are you okay?"

"Don't ask me that." She put her hands over her ears and danced harder, faster. Sweat glistened on her temples.

He reached up to pull her hands down. The alarm bells in his chest had begun to ping. This wasn't just a woman who hadn't been into that night's crop of dance partners. Something was truly weighing on her soul. "Listen, I just want to know if—"

"No!" To his horror, she stopped dead. Her eyes widened and filled with tears until she looked utterly crestfallen. "Stop. You don't understand— Oh, God—"

Without warning, racking sobs seemed to explode from her. She covered her face with her palms and sank in an awkward squat to the dance floor, one knee up, the other bent inward to rest on the worn hardwood. Her shoulders shook with the force of her pain.

Startled, Nate glanced around. This, he hadn't expected. Other dancers started noticing Erin, slowing down to stare and whisper behind their hands. A surge of protectiveness fueled Nate. He squatted and put his arm around her shoulder, leaning in to whisper in her ear.

"Listen. I don't know what's wrong, but I'm going to get you out of here, okay? We'll go outside for some air, get away from all these prying eyes."

All the fight seemed to have seeped out of her, and she acquiesced easily. He helped her to her feet, then sheltered her from the gaping stares as he ushered her from the bar.

Outside, the street was virtually deserted, and the cool black of the October nighttime enveloped them. He led her around the corner of the building to the side, away from the entrance and any on-lookers. People had no shame.

Still sobbing, Erin leaned against the brick exterior and slid to the ground, resting her forehead on her knees. Nate stood awkwardly beside her, letting her cry it—whatever *it* was—out. God knew, she seemed to need it.

When her sobs slowed to hiccups and sniffles, Nate sat on the ground beside her, careful not to touch her. Some primal instinct told him she wouldn't appreciate that sort of consolation.

As her hiccups slowed, then stopped, her whole body seemed to sag. A long period of silence stretched between them. Even with swollen eyes and a red nose, she was lovely. Like a fragile porcelain doll—strong, but at risk of shattering any moment.

"God, I'm…a mess. I'm not usually like this. I'm so sorry," she whispered.

A tender smile lifted one corner of his mouth. "No apology necessary. I didn't mean to make you cry."

She lifted her head, then ran her hands through her hair. "It wasn't you."

What was it? he wondered.

She stared off into the distance, and her chin began to quiver again. Then came the tears, silent this time, but even more forceful for their quietness.

He didn't know what to do.

"Erin...can I give you a ride home?"

Sodium vapor streetlights glistened pinkish-orange in the wet rivulets streaking down her face. She shook her head. "I'm from out of town."

Nate closed his eyes briefly. Of course she was from out of town. That's the way this knight in shining armor stuff usually worked out. He knew that, and yet he kept jumping back into the saddle.

Official verdict: he needed therapy.

"To your hotel, then?"

"I...no. I drove straight through. I mean, I don't have a hotel."

A rock of worry plummeted in his gut. As much as he yearned to bow out gracefully since she didn't seem to want comfort or conversation, he couldn't, in good conscience, let this woman get behind the wheel. Her level of concentration was nil, not to mention the fact that she must be emotionally exhausted. "How far do you have to drive?"

"Too far. But I can do it."

Nate blew out a sigh, turning away to gaze out at the empty street.

"Don't look so worried. It's not your problem. I can take care of myself."

There it was—his easy out. Too bad the bravado in her tone, the intrepid jut of her chin, ensnared him. "Listen, anyone can see you're a strong woman, and I have no doubt you can take care of yourself, and then some, on a regular day. But you're wiped out. You're upset. It's almost 1:00 a.m. You shouldn't drive, and you look smart enough that you probably know that."

She rested her head against the brick wall and closed her eyes. "Everything allegedly looks better in the morning, right?" She shrugged. "I can sleep in my car."

And risk the predators coming back and finding her there, sleeping in a desolate bar parking lot? No freakin' way. Another long pause ensued.

Finally, Nate sighed. "I'm staying at a hotel downtown. Not far from here, actually," he started, regretting this already, wishing he could yank back the eleven words he'd just uttered, but knowing he wouldn't.

She glanced over at him, wary but listening.

That was something, at least.

"Why don't you come and get some sleep there. I'll drive you back here in the morning when you're rested."

Another long pause.

"Why?" she whispered.

Wasn't that obvious? "To pick up your car."

"No. I mean, why are you trying to help?" She searched his face. "You don't even know me."

He laughed, a tired sound. "According to my mom, I'm a born-and-bred rescuer."

"I don't need rescuing."

He ignored that. "Not to mention, I'm a sucker for a crying woman."

"I am *not* a crier," she said, her tone indignant.

"Oh, no." He pierced her with a droll stare. "I can see that."

She glared at him through puffy eyes.

Not wanting to anger her, he winked.

She had the decency to look sheepish as she wiped away her tears. "I mean, I'm not *usually* a crier."

He held her gaze, nodded. "Like I said, you strike me as a self-sufficient woman, but there are days when the strongest of us need a friend. I'm offering my friendship. That's it. No strings."

"There are always strings."

"Wow, you're jaded."

No denial. She eyed him from head to toe. "I don't suppose you're a serial killer or anything, are you? They say serial killers look normal."

"Well, I'm flattered you think I look normal. As for the other, I'm perfectly safe. But I wouldn't expect you to take my word for it." He unhooked his cell phone from his waistband and handed it to her. "Call my mom for a reference, if you need to. Her numbers are in my contacts list under Mom."

Her forehead crinkled with incredulity. "Don't be ridiculous. I can't call your mother in the middle of the night."

"She's an E.R. nurse supervisor and she works graveyards. This is probably her perkiest time of the day."

Erin stared at the cell phone in her hand for several long moments, then flipped it open with her thumb and clicked through his contacts list. He watched as she read the screens for Mom—home, cell, pager and work—then snapped the phone closed and handed it back to him. "Where is area code 702?"

"Las Vegas."

"Are you from there, too?"

"Yes. Born and bred."

"So, why are you here?"

"Business."

She nodded, seeming to ponder this.

Several tense moments passed.

"Do you like animals?" she asked, nailing him with an unflinching stare.

Okay, wow. That came out of nowhere. He cocked his head at her curiously, then opened his phone again. He pressed a few buttons to launch the camera function, then pulled up a photograph of his black cocker spaniel, graying slightly around the muzzle, but still a beauty. "That's my dog. He's nine years old and going strong."

She leaned forward and looked at the picture, her mouth registering the faintest of smiles. "What's his name?"

"Boomer. And—" he clicked through until a photo of a powdery brown, lop-eared rabbit filled the screen "—this is Boomer's pal, Thug. He's just one-year-old."

She gaped at the phone, then faced him, blinking. "You have a bunny named Thug?"

He nodded. "Terrifying, isn't he? He's house-trained. Uses a litter box, and I have to brag that he's quite the neat freak. Not all house-trained rabbits are."

"Huh," she said, wonder in her tone.

Hopeful, he forged ahead. "He and Boomer sleep side by side on Boomer's dog bed. They've done so since Thug was eight weeks old."

"Thug." She paused. "A dog-loving bunny."

"More surprising, really, is the bunny-loving dog."

"Good point." She studied the photo a moment longer, then shook her head and pushed to her feet. "Okay. You win, Nate. Let's go."

Chapter Three

Despite the water bringing out the awful smoke smell again, Erin stood in the stark hotel shower longer than she should have, trying to muster her courage to face the stranger in the other room. It had seemed like a sound decision as they'd driven here, but now, in such close quarters, the second-guessing had begun. Big-time. Her self-consciousness was at an all-time high.

Had she lost her mind?

She'd always been a good judge of character, so it wasn't that she feared Nate anymore. He truly seemed harmless, and she was no idiot. Maybe

Good Samaritans did exist. But nothing mitigated the fact that her decision to take him up on his offer was insanely out of character for her.

Good guy or not, no one in her life knew where the hell she was. No one. She could disappear and wind up on *Cold Case Files* in five years—no leads. They'd show still photos of her with her stupid high school hair, and her family and friends would give tearful, on-screen interviews, pleading for any detail that might crack the case.

That improbability aside, she just didn't head off to hotels or homes—or anywhere—with men, strangers or otherwise. Not since...

The pain stabbed at her again.

Stabbed and stabbed and stabbed.

Oh, God.

How had she managed to avoid dealing with this for so long, only to have it hit her so hard all of a sudden? She took advantage of the shower's loud *whoosh*, leaned her head back, and let her tears come freely, gulping back audible sobs as the water doused her face. She'd cried more in the past few hours than she had in the last decade, and she didn't much like it.

But she had to face facts.

What kind of pathetic life was she living, anyway? Solitary, tormented, getting herself into stupid situations in bars, for God's sake? She threw

herself into work and denial and avoided close relationships like the Unibomber, pretending a
bravado and a "charming snarky humor" she didn't
truly feel. At least not all the time.

This wasn't supposed to be her life.

Bottom line.

She and Kev had been Troublesome Gulch High
School's golden couple. Most likely to marry right
after graduation. Most likely to come to the ten-year
reunion with photos of their two-point-five kids,
and imminent plans to renew their marriage vows.
Solid. Exuberant in their once-in-a-lifetime love
and committed to each other, mind, body and soul.

But, look at her now. Twenty-nine years old, and
she hadn't even kissed, much less made love with,
a single man since Kevin. Couldn't even wrap her
brain around the idea. She wasn't "most likely" to
do jack anymore, except perhaps die alone and
lonely with a fake smile pasted on her face.

Is that what Kevin would've wanted for her?

Was he looking down on her now with pity in
his beautiful green eyes?

She wiped ineffectually at her tears before
turning off the shower. The curtain rings sang
along the metal pole as she pulled the white plastic
aside and groped for a towel. She took her time
smoothing the fluffy terry cloth over the tight, ugly
scar tissue that covered her entire torso, not com-

pletely feeling its roughness, thanks to deadened nerve endings.

As always, she avoided looking into the full-length mirror mounted on the back of the bathroom door. She appreciated her body for what it could do. After all, look at Lexy, who hadn't walked since the accident. Things could be much worse. But still, functional or not, Erin didn't want to glimpse the body she'd never really accepted. At least visually.

It might *be* her, but it didn't *feel* like her.

And yet, the grotesque physical scars from that fire were a mere blip compared to those on her heart.

Wasn't *she* just the total package. Ha.

Before smoothing lotion over her skin, she set out her underwear and the oversized Avalanche T-shirt Nate had thoughtfully picked up for her at the grocery store when he'd stopped for a few toiletries he thought she might need. He'd even bought her a razor—a pink one. She shook her head, one corner of her mouth quivering into a half smile despite her melancholy. Her savior-out-of-nowhere really did seem like a nice guy.

Ugh. What did he think of *her?*

How could she face him?

Her insides bubbled with humiliation.

This whole situation was world-class awkward.

At least, thank goodness, she'd never see him again.

A soft knock on the locked door startled her. She jerked, clutching the towel to her chest before swallowing twice to steady her voice. "Yes?"

"Sorry to bother you. No rush, but a great old movie is available on pay-per-view, *A Guy Named Joe*. Ever heard of it?"

"No."

"Well…it's one of my favorites. World War II flick. If you're interested."

"I…uh…" A movie? This was weirder and weirder. "I'll probably just go to sleep, if that's okay. But I can sleep through anything, so feel free to watch it. Seriously."

"Okay." He paused, but she could tell he was still there. "Are you, um, hungry? I was going to order pizza from room service. They make a pretty good one here."

"No," she said quickly, still frozen in the shower, vulnerable and wanting him to move away from the door so she'd stop feeling so damned… naked. "I'm fine. Thanks."

A pause. "Sure."

She listened, alert, until he was gone. Alone again, she eased out an exhale, dressed quickly, then went through the blow-drying, tooth-brushing, moisturizing routine. She wasn't going for prom queen perfection here. Why would she care what Nate the Savior thought of the way she looked?

She didn't. She was going to bed.

Bed. Ugh.

The land mine zone, as she could see it, stretched between the locked bathroom and the bed. Twenty steps, tops. She wanted to navigate it as quickly and safely as possible, pile herself beneath the covers and slip into oblivion. She wasn't one to take sleeping pills, but if she'd had one, she'd pop it tonight, no questions asked.

Enough stalling. *Now or never.*

She took a deep breath, then eased it out through pursed lips. The lock clicking open sounded like gunfire. She froze again, like a bunny facing a starving rottweiler.

Why was she so edgy? Gee, maybe because she'd humiliated herself in front of a total stranger, and now she had to spend the night in his room?

Nate glanced up with a faint smile as she entered the main room. The phone rested between his shoulder and ear, and he was busy ordering extra this and extra that, thin crust and a side of whatever.

Erin forced her standard fake smile back, then climbed into her bed on the far side. Safety. Thank God she'd made it. She covered herself chin high, chilled to her marrow and shivering, despite the extra-long steamy shower.

Nate hung up. "I ordered an extra large in case you change your mind."

Small talk. Bleh. Oh yeah—that's what strangers did in excruciatingly squirm-worthy situations such as this. "That was nice of you."

He lifted his chin in the direction of the bathroom. "How was the shower?"

"Fine." She forged ahead. "Listen, I didn't thank you for picking all the stuff up for me."

"Yes, you did. You're more than welcome." He stood, glancing toward the bathroom. "Think I'll take a quick one before the pizza gets here. They said it would be thirty minutes, but you know how it goes."

Her mind wasn't on pizza delivery schedules at all at the moment. She twisted her mouth to the side, guilt squeezing her breathless.

Nate lifted an eyebrow. "What's wrong?"

"I didn't realize you wanted to shower. I hope I didn't hog all the hot water."

He grinned. "Not to worry, I grew up with a bath-loving mom and three sisters. I'm used to cold."

Yeah, that didn't assuage anything. She pulled her bottom lip between her teeth. "No, really. I shouldn't have stayed in there so long. It's your room, and—"

"Stop."

They stared at each other.

"Erin, you needed the time. I get that, okay? Besides, these big hotels never run out of hot water."

Feeling slightly better, she relaxed—at least as much as she could when everything was so formal and clumsy and surreal between them.

"Let's make a deal. You stop saying 'thanks' and 'sorry' for the rest of the night. Okay?"

"I'll try."

"Good enough." Nate halted at the end of her bed en route the bathroom. He snapped his fingers, then fished his wallet out of his back pocket. "If, for some strange reason, the pizza arrives while I'm in there, I've got cash for a tip." He lobbed it onto the end of her bed.

Her body went cold as she stared at the worn leather. It seemed too intimate, this wallet so perfectly molded to his backside.

"Now what's wrong?"

She flicked a hand toward it. "I...I can't just dig through your wallet."

He blinked. Poker face. "Sure you can. I just said you could."

She shook her head. "B-but, that's not the point. We just met." She groaned. "This is really uncomfortable. I could be some coldhearted criminal taking advantage of your kindness."

"Are you?"

"No. But that's not the point."

"I can solve this. Answer one question."

She waited.

"Do you like animals?" he asked, playfulness in his gentle eyes.

"You can't use my questions against me."

"Why not? It worked for you." He spread his arms wide. "See?"

She rolled her eyes. "You are way too trusting."

He laughed softly. "Somehow, you just don't strike me as the criminal type."

"I suppose that's comforting." She swallowed thickly, eyeing the wallet as though it were a rattlesnake poised to strike. "Just hurry, okay? Then I won't have to touch it at all, which will make us both feel better. Think, quick shower."

He shrugged. "I'm a guy. How else do we shower except quickly?"

She'd succumbed to a slice of pizza after all—the aroma had gotten to her. Tummy full, she rolled over to leave Nate to his movie, circa 1943, or something like that.

Weird.

She didn't think guys liked old movies, not that she was any expert on guys. And she was probably being grossly stereotypical. Then again, this was a war flick.

Or so he alleged.

Turned out the WWII fighter pilot main character gets killed on a mission, and is forced to come back as another young fighter pilot's guardian angel, only to watch while the guy falls in love with his mourning fiancée.

Yeah. *Not* a war picture.

Partway through, she couldn't contain her curiosity, so she rolled over to watch.

Nate glanced at her. "Is the TV keeping you awake?"

"No. I just…this film seems familiar somehow."

He turned his attention back to the screen. "Richard Dreyfuss and Holly Hunter starred in the remake. *Always*. Late eighties, I think, and a whole lot different. But based on the same story."

A vice gripped her stomach, while her eyes were transfixed on the television. Of course. *Always* was one of the many sad movies about loss of love that she'd studiously avoided. They never failed to rekindle her melancholy to an unbearable burn. What were the odds? Pretty damn good, actually, since *every* sad movie affected her that way.

Ghost? Forget it.

"Seen it?"

She shot a glance at him. "Excuse me?"

"*Always*. Just wondering if you'd seen the remake. Maybe that's why this one's familiar."

"Oh." She dropped her gaze. "Yes." Unfortunately.

"Original version's better."

Great.

She pondered his earlier description of the movie, amused in spite of herself. "Nate, there's something you should know," she said, her tone deliberately grave.

He held up the remote. "Should I pause it?"

"Maybe."

He did. "Okay, what's up?"

She leveled him with a serious gaze. "This may come as a shock, but *A Guy Named Joe* isn't a war flick. Hate to blow your cover."

He did a double take, aiming a thumb toward the still screen. "Sure it is. You saw the uniforms. The planes."

"Doesn't matter. It's a love story. An old-school chick flick. Practically a precursor to *Love Story* itself."

Nate sighed. "Okay. Truth time?"

"Hit me."

"I know it's a love story. But being the only male in my household, it was the closest I ever came to an action flick of any kind." He eyed her from the side. "My sisters—"

"What are their names?" She found herself suddenly curious about this guy. Sisters? A mom? Boomer and Thug? Like, he had a whole life beyond this hellish night, which struck her as so…strange.

"In order, Flannery, Colette and Piper. We're all about a year apart, and I'm second in the lineup, smack between Flannery and Colette."

"Cool names."

"My mom's creative."

"Are they married?"

"Nope. Not even Mom's remarried."

"Where's your dad?" she blurted, before realizing it was a fairly rude question.

He shrugged, as though it didn't matter a bit. "Not really a part of our lives."

"Ever?"

"Well, I don't remember him."

She felt a pang of compassion before another thought struck. "Wait a sec. You're not married, are you?"

He castigated her wordlessly. Those eyes of his could speak volumes.

She held up both palms in surrender. "Just asking. Because if you were my husband, away on business, and you brought some woman back to your hotel room, I wouldn't be happy. To put it mildly. Even if she was a whackjob and you were just being nice."

He bonked his head on the headboard. "So *you're* married. Great. Is some burly guy going to come after me with a sawed-off shotgun?"

She widened her eyes. "Me? No, never. It was just an example."

"That's a relief." He pointed toward the entertainment center. "So, back to why I'm watching a chick flick and calling it a war movie."

"Yes." She inclined her head. "Sorry for the nosy interruption. It just struck me as interesting that you have sisters."

He laughed. "What—you thought I sprang out of nowhere in that bar?"

"Superheroes usually do."

He scoffed. "I'm no superhero. Anyway, it's okay. The interruption, I mean. I like talking about my family, and they're the whole point anyway. The truth is, I was outnumbered growing up when it came to picking movies. And Mom took my sisters' side not because she favored them, but because she didn't want us to watch violence anyway."

"Ah. Well, no shame in that."

"So *you* say. I had to keep some kind of street cred with my buddies," he said. "So I started 're-defining' the movies we watched. *Steel Magnolias?* I've seen it about fifty times. I could probably quote dialogue, a skill that doesn't go over big on the basketball court."

A short laugh burst from Erin, the sound unfamiliar, almost painful on this night. It shocked her so much, she reached up and covered her mouth.

He smiled, the expression etching lines around

his eyes, which were a beautiful shade of turquoise—a great contrast against his black hair and tanned skin. "So, all my ugly secrets aside, will you humor me and let me call it a war flick?"

She cleared her throat. "Sure. Go back to your war flick. I'm going to try to sleep."

"Good night."

She rolled over and settled in. He still hadn't started the movie. She could almost feel his eyes boring into her back. "Nate?"

"Yeah?"

"Did I ever thank you for helping me?" she asked, without turning around.

"I thought we had a deal about that."

"Oh, yeah. Sorry."

"Ah, that was part of the deal, too."

"Right. No more talking."

A pause. "'Night, Erin."

"Good night."

She tried—really tried—to fall asleep. Tried to buzz the movie dialogue out of her brain. Tried to forget. It hadn't worked. By the time the credits rolled, Erin sort of wanted to die. Not literally. That was one of those oft-used flippant comments she tried to never think or say, if only out of respect for her friends who hadn't had the chance. But everything about her trauma, everything she'd hoped to get in check, had ripped open again, a fresh, un-cleaned wound.

Her back still to Nate, she'd started pretending to sleep about forty-five minutes earlier. The last thing she wanted was a compare-and-contrast conversation about the two versions of this godawful, heartbreaking movie.

The television clicked off, then she heard Nate rustling in his own bed. "Erin?" he asked, softly.

She squeezed her eyes shut and remained still.

Obviously buying her pathetic attempt at fake sleep, Nate doused the bedside lamp. The last thing she heard was his sigh as he punched his pillow and settled in.

The self-lambasting started almost immediately.

She should've told him good-night. Asked him if he still loved his movie after having seen it a million times. She should've gone the give route with this guy, instead of take, take, take.

How hard would it have been to extend a hand of friendship, the way he had?

This wasn't all about her, after all.

She wasn't generally so selfish.

Oh well. It wasn't as if he expected her to act like a normal, sane woman after the crazy evening they'd shared. She might as well leave it alone. After tomorrow, they'd go their separate ways forever. This night of a thousand embarrassments would fade with time until she was nothing but an anecdote he shared with his guy friends during those "what not to do" conversations.

Realistically, in the movie of her life, Nate the Savior was an extra.

Walk on. Walk off. No lines.

Her bloodcurdling scream ripped him from sleep. Nate tore out of his bed and smacked on the lamp, blinking into the glaring light. His glance shot from one side of the room to the other, looking for the intruder, the attacker.

Empty.

Relief flowed through him as he slowly realized the enigmatic woman sharing his hotel room was simply in the throes of a wicked nightmare.

Somehow, not surprising.

He blew out a long breath and ran his fingers through his hair. He yearned to awaken her, but he didn't want her to think he was breaching boundaries, crossing over to her side of the room.

And yet, the nightmare still had her in its talons.

He held back, watching as her scream devolved to panting, then moved into racking sobs and nearly incoherent babble. It sounded like she was saying, "Why me?" or "Why not me?" Or maybe "Whiny?"—not that any of it made sense. Beneath the top sheet—she'd kicked off all the other covers—she curled into a fetal ball, rocking as she cried.

He couldn't take this.

She'd just have to forgive his intrusion.

Sitting carefully on the edge of her bed, he reached out and touched her shoulder. "Erin," he whispered.

Nothing.

He cleared his throat and spoke louder. "Erin."

She sucked in a huge gulp of air as she battled to a sitting position, hair wild, eyes disoriented as she searched the unfamiliar surroundings. "K-kev?"

Kev? He shook his head. "It's me, Nate."

"Oh." She ran a shaky hand through her hair, averting her gaze. "Oh. Shoot."

"You were having a nightmare."

"Yeah, I uh…I have them sometimes." Blotches of color rose to her cheeks. "I didn't mean to disturb you. Again." She leaned forward for the disheveled covers, pulling them up to her chest and tucking them firmly beneath her arms.

"I didn't wake you for an apology." He waited until she looked up at him, her luminous eyes troubled, but so strong. God, something about this woman touched him, right where he lived. "Are you okay?"

The pause seemed interminable.

She pulled her quivering bottom lip in between her teeth. "I don't know. Actually, no."

He lifted his arms and let them drop. "Please talk to me. It's torture watching you go through this when I don't even know what *this* is."

"It's complicated, that's all." She pushed all ten fingers into the front of her hair and held them there for a few moments. "Too complicated for strangers."

Is that what they were? He didn't feel like a stranger anymore. He took a risk, reaching forward to grab her hand.

"Look at it this way. I'm an uninvolved party. Use me as a sounding board. There has to be something I can do." He watched for several long moments while she stared down at the bed coverings.

Her throat tightened with a swallow, once, then again. When she finally spoke, her words managed to sound both stiff and broken. "I don't want to talk about it. It's ancient history, really. But, will you…" She pressed her lips together and shook her head.

"What?" he prompted. "Will I what?"

Her sidelong glance was humiliated and apologetic. "Just lie here with me?"

Surprise riddled through him.

Her complexion blazed red. "I know it seems weird, but…"

"No, it's—" Of all the requests in the world, that

wasn't the one he'd imagined he'd hear. Ever. It actually stunned him silent.

"Please?" she whispered, a wobbly sound.

Don't be an idiot, his brain warned. *Do not get in bed with this woman.* "If you're sure."

"I'm not sure of anything. Except that I don't feel like being alone right now." Fumbling and formal, they moved side by side on the bed, her beneath the covers, him on top. For a few agonizing moments, they remained that way. Staring at the ceiling. Like corpses.

How could this possibly be helping her?

She swallowed. Moistened her lips with a quick flick of her tongue. "It's okay. You can, um, get in."

He turned toward her. "Erin, I don't know—"

"I just need to feel someone close, that's all. I'm not going to do anything to you."

More's the pity. He studied her lovely, if heartbroken, profile for several moments, then moved beneath the covers. The XXL T-shirt he'd bought her covered most of her, but her firm, shapely legs felt smooth and soft against him. Exquisite torture, this good guy stuff. His danger signals wailed louder.

Erin cleared her throat. "May I…ugh, this is absurd…may I put my head on your shoulder?"

"Of course."

She rose up, then stopped, looking down at him through wide eyes. "Oh, God. Never mind.

This was an idiotic idea. I never should've put you in this pos—"

"Shh." He slid his arm beneath her shoulders and urged her head onto his shoulder, smelling the strawberry scent of her hair. "It's okay. Friends, right?"

"Right."

"Just try to get some sleep." He reached over and snapped the lamp off, enclosing them in the safety of darkness once again.

He felt her nod, closed his eyes.

After a moment, she whispered, "Nate?"

He opened one eye. "Mmm-hmm?"

"You're a good guy. Your mom should be proud."

"She is. But thank you for saying so." He smiled into the inky night and snuggled her closer. They might be strangers, and their meeting unconventional, but damned if she didn't feel absolutely perfect in his arms.

Chapter Four

The idea came to her in a burst.

A ridiculous idea, but one she couldn't let go of. She hadn't been able to sleep, the feeling of being cradled by a man so absolutely foreign. But not bad. Not bad at all. She lay there in the darkness pressed against Nate's shoulder, smelling the clean, soapy manliness of his skin, and trying to make sense of the myriad thoughts swirling through her head.

Kevin.

Her life.

The accident.

Nate.

She thought about Brody Austin, and how he'd been able to overcome his emotional wounds from their horrible prom night. Since he'd returned to Troublesome Gulch, Erin had always rationalized that he was much braver than she, able to suck it up and take a leap into the scary unknown. No net. No anything.

Maybe, in reality, having the guts to return had simply been his first step.

One step that had led to another, and another, and another, until he'd fought his way out of the darkness into the joy that epitomized his new life. What was that old saying? The journey of a thousand miles begins with a single step?

She could take that single step.

Right now. Tonight. With Nate.

If she were brave enough.

Her heart pounded just considering the absurd idea percolating inside her addled brain. Since she'd only been with Kevin, she'd obviously never indulged in a one-night stand. But, even in theory, it totally wasn't her thing.

That's what made this idea so…

Still, if she didn't make some sort of an effort soon, she would surely die without ever loving again. Without ever having sex again, and that idea made her sad.

This possible tryst with Nate didn't need to be mind-blowing. Neither of them needed to impress the other. It would be more like ripping off a Band-Aid, at least for her. The quicker, the better. Just get it done.

Surely Nate would be willing. What guy wouldn't want a little no-strings sex? For a brief moment, hope bubbled inside her. Then, *Pop! Pop! Pop!* Gone.

Forget it. She was an idiot.

People didn't *do* this sort of thing. They didn't even contemplate it. Did they?

She adjusted her head on Nate's shoulder, studying his strong profile, admiring the sweep of dark lashes on his cheeks, watching his sculpted chest rise and fall with deep, restful breaths.

Weird, yes, but it wouldn't be horrible. She found him genuinely attractive—a fact that stunned her. She hadn't even looked twice at a guy since Kevin.

Could she do it?

Tentatively, she reached her fingers up and traced his squared jawline which bore a hint of stubble, not at all unattractive. A sudden urge to feel its roughness against the smooth skin of her face and neck overtook her. She'd ignored her own sexuality for so long, and suddenly it reared up, demanding attention.

Now.

Nate stirred. She froze.

For several long moments, she didn't even draw a breath. But he didn't wake up, thank God.

She eased the pent-up breath out through her lips and continued her exploration. Gentle as butterfly wings, she moved her fingers down to his smooth chest, testing her resolve. Could she touch another man? Even for therapeutic reasons? Laying her palm against his warm skin, she smoothed it lightly down his sculpted abs, surprised by the ferocity of the yearning swirling deep within her, in a place she'd believed long dead.

Her hand traced his six-pack. One-two. Three-four. Five-six, and so close to the danger zone. She yearned to touch him there, too—

Quick as a viper, Nate's palm wrapped around her wrist.

She sucked in air.

For a moment, no one spoke.

"What are you doing?" he asked, his voice alert, despite being gravelly with sleep.

"I…" She paused, forced a swallow. What could she say? *I'm trying to figure out if I could stand to make love with you?* Now *that* was a world-class pickup line.

"Erin."

Now or never. *Answer the man.*

It'll be okay, Brody had told her. But it would

never be okay if she kept on doing exactly what she'd been doing for the past decade-plus.

One night.

One hurdle crossed.

That's all she needed.

Nate wanted to help her. He'd said so himself.

"Erin," Nate said again, a bit more adamantly. "I asked you what you're doing."

"I was, ah, touching you."

"Okay. Why?"

She shored up all her courage. "Well, the thing is, I've been thinking. And I want you to make love to me."

Dead.

Freakin'.

Silence.

After what seemed like interminable nothingness, during which all she could hear was the percussion of her pulse, Nate reached over and flicked on the lamp. It was worse, seeing him in the light after just having voiced her insane suggestion.

Apparently, he was equally stunned. His eyes narrowed. "What did you say?"

"I said—" *deep breath…courage* "—I want to make love. With you. Now."

Nate stared at her as though she were insane, then released a sound that was half laugh, half gasp. He ran his fingers through his hair. "Where is this coming from? An hour ago, you called us strangers."

"I know, but—"

"Is this some sort of a game?"

Anger tinged his words, and her throat tightened. She hadn't expected anger. "No. No. It's just—I can explain—"

"Yeah, you'd better explain."

Self-conscious to the max, she moistened her lips. This was, arguably, the most mortifying moment of her life. "Look, we're both adults. I went through something…sort of traumatic today." Her glance slid toward the digital clock. "Yesterday, actually. And I just need to feel alive, Nate."

Another disbelieving stare. "You want to make love with a so-called total stranger to feel alive?"

"No strings," she said, recalling his words. Maybe he thought she was trying to trap him. "I promise." She reached out tentatively and ran her fingers through his hair, relieved to see the expression in his eyes darken with desire.

She could see him fighting it off, and the desire turned to disgust. "No strings." He huffed. "That's what you think I'm worried about?"

"Well, I—"

His body stiffened. "And here I thought we'd started to get to know each other."

"We have," she rushed to say, propping herself

up on one elbow so she could look at him directly. "That's why I thought—"

"That I'd be your perfect candidate?" He whipped back the covers and stood, eyes flashing. "Guess what, Erin? I'm not the kind of guy to go in for an easy lay because it's offered. If that's what you were looking for, I could've left you at the bar."

"I didn't want—" She sat up, tugging at the bottom of her T-shirt. "That's not it. God!" She put her face in her hands. "Never mind," came her muffled words. "It was a stupid proposition. Forget I ever said anything."

She'd never been more embarrassed.

With a sigh, Nate sat tentatively on the edge of her bed. "What is going on with you? Who are you?"

"I'm nobody." She couldn't keep the bereft tone from her words. "I'm a sham."

He reached out and stroked her hair. "Not true."

"No, it is." She tried to focus, to ignore how his touch made her feel. "Want to know something ridiculous?"

He waited.

"I haven't made love with anyone for more than eleven years," she whispered, her voice laced with shame. "I haven't even kissed anyone."

He blinked twice. "By choice?"

She hiked one shoulder. "I guess. No. I don't know."

"Then why? Surely you've had interest. You're a beautiful woman."

"I'm not beautiful. Besides, it's a long story."

He propped himself back on two pillows and crossed his arms. "I've got nothing but time. After your shocking suggestion, I guarantee I'm not going to be able to go back to sleep. So we might as well talk."

She blew out her frustration. Tucked her hair behind her ears. "I was engaged," she said, in a monotone. "My fiancé died. Some people can recover from trauma, others struggle. End of story."

The pause stretched out, riddled with his attempts to absorb all this and her sadness, to find the right words when none existed.

"I'm sorry," he said finally, his tone husky.

She huffed out a humorless laugh. "Me, too."

"Did you love him?"

"With my whole heart and soul."

"Come here." Nate pulled her into his arms and cradled her head against his shoulder, smoothing his palm down her back. "It's not that I wouldn't want to make love to you under normal circumstances. You're sexy. Sweet."

"Celibate."

He ignored that. "But, Erin, despite the fact that

I'm not a one-night-stand guy, I don't even have protection. I don't carry that kind of stuff 'just in case.' That's not the way I live."

She lifted her head to glance up at him. "Which is what makes the whole thing perfect."

He raised his eyebrows, waiting.

"I'm safe, Nate. I can't get pregnant, and I haven't been with anyone in so long, I'm a virtual virgin."

He shook his head at her self-deprecation. "What about me? What do you know about me?"

Her gaze slanted to the side. "I know you don't carry protection 'just in case.' I know you're an exceptional man, a caring man. You took me from a potentially catastrophic situation when there was nothing whatsoever in it for you. I know you'd tell me if I was in any danger at all."

He mulled over that. "True. For the record, I do get tested, and I'm safe. But that's not the point."

"What's the point then?"

"Lovemaking is special, Erin. It's not something you tick off your To-Do List."

Man, he nailed that on the head. What he didn't understand was, sometimes you just had to tackle that damned list. She groaned. "Okay, I *want* to make love with you. Does that help?"

"Not exactly. It might, if you were the least bit convincing."

She shouldered away from him. "Look. I

haven't wanted any man so much as near me for more than a decade, and then you come along and I get all these crazy ideas. It's not like I've been propositioning every guy who comes along."

"Then why me?" he whispered.

There were no words. No reasonable explanation. Instead, she stretched up and kissed his lips softly, which felt strange, foreign, but not horrible. He tasted good, like mint and man. Safe. When he didn't protest, she deepened the kiss, venturing some exploration with her tongue, nibbling at his bottom lip.

He groaned. Obviously tried not to, but it escaped anyway, and he kissed her back. For several long moments, they simply explored each other's mouths. His hands moved up to cup her face gently, and an unexpected storm of desire ripped through her. Wait. This was supposed to be a first step, nothing more.

Yet, it seemed she truly wanted this man.

How could that be?

He wasn't Kevin, but she ached for him. She yearned to feel Nate's weight on top of her, him pushing into her. Her body throbbed. She knew he wasn't comfortable with this, but he just had to—

"Please," she whispered, moist and warm against his lips.

He pulled back, studied her face. "Why can't you get pregnant?"

"An injury," she hedged.

"That's rough."

"I don't care." She leaned in to kiss him again, this time brazenly spreading her palms on his chest.

"Erin," he breathed against her mouth between kisses. "I don't do this kind of thing. For the record."

"Neither do I. For the record. So let's do it together and call it a friendly aberration."

After hesitation, he eased her back on the pillows and started to pull up her T-shirt.

She sucked in a breath, holding it down. "W-wait."

His eyes glittered with scorn. "Let me guess. Second thoughts already?"

"No. No. But, can I…can I leave it on?"

He cocked his head to the side. "Why?"

"It's just been so long."

He studied her, the uncertainty clear in his gaze.

Afraid he'd call it off, she guided his hand down to her bikini underwear instead, urging his fingers inside, though it was excruciatingly difficult to be so brazen.

He caressed her, closing his eyes as he sucked in a breath. "You're so wet."

"I want this, Nate," she said, trying to convince herself as much as she tried to convince him. "I want you. Can't you see? Feel?"

He slipped one finger inside her—an utter surprise. She gasped, bucking instinctively to deepen the connection. The force of her desire floored her.

His breaths coming quicker now, he eased his finger out of her body, then slid her underwear down her legs.

She kicked them off. Shy, but wanting to take this step, she opened her legs for him, watching as he removed the sweatpants he'd worn to bed.

Oh, he clearly wanted her, too.

The sight of him quickened her pulse. The dull throb intensified at her center. She reached for him, wanting to feel his length in her hand. Instead, he pressed his body against hers, holding off some of his weight with his elbows.

"Tell me you're sure about this."

Not at all. "I'm sure."

"Tell me we're not making a mistake."

Who could say? "We're not."

"I am safe, Erin," he reassured. "I'm a good guy. I'd never put you into a bad situation."

She squirmed against him. "If I had any doubt whatsoever, we wouldn't be here like this, trust me. I just…please."

"Please what?"

"I want you inside me," she whispered shyly.

He leaned his forehead against hers, their gazes locked. "It makes no sense, but I want it, too. Even if I don't understand your reasoning. Or mine. I don't know you, but I feel like I've known you forever."

A rubber band of guilt snapped against her skin. His genuineness stung. Obviously, what he felt for her was mere lust. They'd only just met. But his wanting was sincere. Hers was simply that first step toward getting her life back. Wasn't it?

Regardless, tomorrow they'd go their separate ways, each having gotten what they needed, so what did it matter?

She rubbed against his hardness. "Make love to me."

"If you don't stop that, there's no going back."

"I don't want to go back." She reached down between their bodies and wrapped her palm around him, guiding the tip of his penis toward the throb that had intensified to the point that it didn't seem to want to stop. "Now."

"Erin."

"Now."

Gently, but firmly, he pushed into her. Deeply, all the way. For a moment, they stayed locked that way, and he closed his eyes. "God, you feel incredible."

"It's been a long time."

"I'll be gentle."

Some feral part of her quaked. "Don't. Please. I don't want gentle. Not tonight."

She felt his pulse quicken inside her as he stared into her eyes, and then he did her bidding.

Hard. Fast. Deep. Thorough.

Nate proved to be an amazing lover. He caressed her breasts to aching points through the shirt and never complained that she wouldn't fully undress. He awakened her body in ways she hadn't thought possible.

Fear quivered inside her. Why did it feel as though this was turning into more than she'd bargained for?

Pushing away her alarm, Erin gave herself over to the sensations, rising to meet his thrusts, wanting more, more, more. She felt like the first crocus bloom, bursting through the graying snow after an extended, cold winter.

Silent tears crept out the sides of her eyes, rolling down to tickle her ears. She wanted to believe it was because of Kevin, and partly it was. He was no longer her *only,* and that saddened her to the depths of her soul.

But she also knew she was going to creep out of this room the moment Nate succumbed to sleep, leaving no trace. She would never see him again, and somehow, that cracked the only part of her heart that hadn't already been shattered.

She cried out with her explosive climax, wrapping her legs around Nate's waist and reveling in the feeling of his pulsing release inside her.

"Are you okay?" he gasped.

"Yes."

"Did I hurt you?"

"Not at all." She stretched up to kiss him.

"Good." He kissed her back, passionately. "Good." A pause. "Erin. Honey, I—"

"Shh." She laid a finger across his lips. "Let's not ruin it with words. Let it be what it is, okay? Be in the moment."

He settled on top of her, both of them panting, and a part of her wanted to pull him close and keep him there. Inside her. Around her. On top of her. Forever.

She hadn't expected that.

Dear God, she hadn't expected Nate.

Morning's golden glow shone through his eyelids, awakening him. His mind moved to last night, and a slow smile spread his lips. His body felt spent, his mind soothed. He opened his eyes and let them adjust to the brightness of the new day, then he turned over to greet—

But, she wasn't there.

He pulled the covers back and sat up. "Erin?"

No answer.

Standing, he stretched his arms over his head and yawned as he walked toward the bathroom. Empty. Only when he turned back toward the disheveled bed did he notice the note scribbled on a hotel notepad.

Please understand.

He stood frozen, staring at it, pulse pounding in his temples. He should've known. Should've been prepared for this. So why did it hurt so damn much? Crossing to the bed, Nate sat, and picked up the only bit of Erin he had left.

A goodbye.

Chapter Five

Two months later...

"Mystery solved," the doctor said, as she entered her office bearing a file. "You're pregnant."

Erin gaped at her longtime doctor, the incomprehensible announcement ringing in her ears. "But, I can't be. I came in with the flu."

Dr. Kipfer laughed. Rounding the expansive cherrywood desk, she tossed the file down onto her blotter and sat. "Actually, you came in confused. That flu you have? We in the biz refer to it as morning sickness." She winked.

Erin's heart drummed. She shook her head. "No. It's impossible."

The doctor frowned, perplexed. "Do you mean you haven't had sex? False positives can happen."

Erin's skin flamed. "No, well, I...not that. But, I'm not able to get pregnant. Because of the burns."

The doc steepled her hands on her desk and lowered her chin. "Who told you that? The burn treatment center?"

Erin felt more stupid by the moment. "Um, no, actually." She laid a palm on her still-flat tummy that somehow felt different now. "To be honest, I just assumed. You've seen my scarring."

"Scars on the skin don't always translate to organ damage. Clearly, in your case, your organs are fine."

"Oh." Pregnant. Holy hell. She gulped. "How, um...how far along am I?"

As if she didn't know.

She knew the exact night, practically the exact moment she'd conceived. In fact, she'd spent the last two months trying to convince herself that leaving under cover of darkness, without so much as a thank-you, had been the right thing to do. Now she wasn't so sure. Fitful dreams about Nate, a man so kind and selfless, had haunted her nights. Guilt ate away at her days. And the memories. Oh, the memories....

"Eight weeks," Doc said—no surprise. "You've

got a long way to go, and you're considered high risk, so we're going to monitor you very closely."

Erin's heart squeezed for Nate. She didn't even know his last name. Finding him was likely impossible. Probably a blessing in disguise, since she'd assured him she couldn't get pregnant and then bailed like a coward the moment he'd drifted off into dreamland. Whether she carried his child or not, she was probably the last person he'd ever want to see.

Still, *God,* he deserved to know.

That fact weighed on her soul, dampening what should've been an exciting—if scary—moment. The baby was his, too.

She shook off the thoughts. There were so many practicalities to discuss—why focus on what she couldn't control? "What about my skin? I mean, the stretching?" Surely her scar tissue wouldn't accommodate the growth of a fetus. She cringed at the thought.

Dr. Kipfer tilted her head to the side, her blond bob swinging forward to brush along her shoulder. "Well, that's why we have to keep an eye on things. A lot of it will be your responsibility."

Erin's palms grew damp. "Meaning?"

"Your skin will accommodate for some stretching by pulling from your back. The body is amazing that way. But you cannot gain a lot of weight with this baby, Erin," the doctor said, her tone sober. "Twenty pounds, absolute max." She blinked across the desk without an iota of judgment in her expression. "Assuming, of course, you plan to see this pregnancy through to full term."

Erin reeled as though she'd been slapped. She'd had one baby torn from her by an unlucky twist of fate. No way would she ever voluntarily give up another. "Of course. My God, I wouldn't think of—" She couldn't even say it.

Dr. Kipfer held up both palms and smiled. "Just making sure. I don't like to assume. And whatever you'd choose to do, as your doctor, I'd support you."

"Thank you. But, I want this baby." And, she did. She hadn't expected how ferociously. They felt like an inseparable duo already.

"Well, then. I'd say congratulations are in order. You're going to be a mama."

Mama. Her head swirled in wonder. Erin half laughed, half cried. She never imagined this, and part of her keened with the knowledge that it wasn't Kevin's baby. Then again, Nate…

Stop. Be in the moment.

Excitement sprouted a beautiful little bud inside her heart. She wanted to dash out and shop for all the tiny clothes and precious things to furnish a nursery, but she was getting way ahead of herself. Questions, worries and logistical plans filled her brain until she couldn't think straight. The biggest of which was, "What about work?"

"Yes, that." Dr. Kipfer quirked her mouth to the side apologetically. "You'll have to take a medical leave earlier than most pregnant firefighters."

"What does that mean? How much earlier?"

"Get ready to talk to your fire chief. I'll want you off work and resting at home from twenty weeks through delivery. Eighteen weeks, if you can manage it."

"Eighteen weeks!" Dismay gripped Erin. She did, after all, have to support this child on her own. She hoped she had enough sick time banked, or she'd have to request donations from her coworkers. Ick. "That's four and a half months of bed rest."

The doctor held up a finger. "Now, I didn't say bed rest. We can't risk any extra weight gain, so you'll have to continue to exercise. But you're certainly not going to be out there fighting fires or doing any heavy lifting."

"But, that's my job. I have to earn money."

"What about the father?" Dr. Kipfer asked, softly. "Any help from that end?"

Erin merely shook her head.

"You *do* want a healthy birth, right?"

"Of course."

"Then, get used to the idea. Do what you have

to. Friends, family." She gave her a sympathetic smile. "I know you're not one to ask for help, Erin, but now's the time, okay?"

Erin bit her bottom lip, thinking. "Can I do some light-duty work? Administrative assignments?"

"Let's see how things go."

At Erin's disappointed expression, the doctor added, "Look at it this way. For the next seven months, your body absolutely belongs to that baby, and he or she makes every decision about it."

"Wow. I never thought about it like that."

"Sounds extreme, but it's worth it, trust me." The doctor glanced at photographs of her own four children, displayed on the corner of her desk. "And not to worry. After the birth, that new little soul will give everything back. Except, of course, your heart."

Erin laughed nervously. "I think he already has that."

Dr. Kipfer grinned. "Welcome to mommyhood."

After Erin got used to the idea of being pregnant, it took a week to shore up enough courage to tell her parents, a month for her girl-friends to stop squealing every time they saw her, three months before they stopped grilling her about the identity of the father, and five months before her forced "no work" policy drove her to the absolute brink of institutionalization.

She'd done everything Dr. Kipfer asked of her—eating better than she ever had, exercising regularly, taking it easy. She'd kept her weight gain to just nineteen pounds so far, yet she still felt like an unwieldy Winnebago moving through the world. She'd never bumped into so many things in her life.

The fire chief, a father and grandfather himself, flat-out ordered her to stay home once she reached eighteen weeks, even though the pregnancy was proceeding normally and the fetus seemed strong. Now, with two months to go before delivery, she simply had to get out and do something non-baby-related before her brain up and died.

Before she'd had to ease up, she'd taken care of things full force. The nursery was finished, furnished and fine. She'd decluttered and organized her entire house to within an inch of its life. All her flower beds were planted, and there wasn't a speck of dirt or disarray to be found in her garage—a miracle in itself. Not only that, but she'd kept a daily pregnancy diary to give to her child one day.

Three volumes and counting.

It had gotten so bad that Finn, a dog who'd suffered from separation anxiety, mind you, was actually sick of her company. Pack animal or not, the poor dog wanted his space. She could hardly blame the big guy, because she'd been getting on her *own* nerves for months.

As far as the impending labor, Cagney was glee-fully acting as her Lamaze coach, and her birth plan had been written and revised to anal-retentive perfection. Her hospital bag was packed and had taken up permanent residence next to her front door. The phone tree was set up, printed out, dis-persed and tested.

Now, the only thing left was thinking about Nate and wallowing in guilt about everything he was missing. She'd gone so far as to Google "Nate" and "Las Vegas" in the inane hopes of stumbling across him, but the results were too daunting. None of the listings stuck out to her, and no way was she calling hundreds of men to tell them they might be her baby's father.

She'd even sucked up her pride and tried the hotel in Denver where they'd created this new little life together. Unfortunately, privacy policies pre-vented them from giving her any info, and no matter how much she pleaded, they wouldn't budge.

Insanity lurked on the horizon waiting to grab her. Something had to give.

Knowing she was likely in for a lecture, she nevertheless drove to the Fire Department head-quarters, bypassed the department secretary and knocked on the chief's door.

Her throat tightened as she waited.

With a quizzical expression on his face, Chief

John Dresden pulled open the door, then broke into a huge smile. "DeLuca! What are you doing out of your house?" He pulled her into a fatherly bear hug.

"I'm allowed to leave my house, Chief."

He held her at arm's length and studied her. "You look well, you look well. But really, why take any chances?" He ushered her in, actually holding her elbow as she sat in one of his visitors' chairs. She smirked, but didn't comment. The grandpa in him was really coming out, full force.

"To what do I owe this nice surprise?"

"Just wanted to say hi," she lied, in a breezy tone.

"Come on. I know you better than that."

After he'd crossed behind the desk and sat down, she blew out her frustration. "The thing is, Chief, I'm going stark-raving mad sitting around at home. I can't do it anymore. So, I've come to request…okay, beg for…some light-duty work. My doctor says it's okay."

He tilted his chin down. "Now, come on. You only have a few more weeks to go."

She barked out a painful laugh. "That's easy for you to say, but it's eight weeks. Eight, which is technically more than 'a few.' And I've been stuck in my house for fourteen weeks already. That's three and a half months, in case you don't feel like doing the math."

"Well, don't you have things to prepare?"

"All due respect, sir, but are you kidding?" She spread her arms wide. "The nursery was done my first month at home. I won't even go into all the rest of my frighteningly obsessive nesting activities, but let me just say I actually alphabetized my pantry the other day, which is so not me. I'm scaring myself. You have to give me a small assignment. I don't know what I'll do if you say no."

He steepled his fingers, resting them against his lips. "I don't know," he said, finally, stretching his neck side to side. "I don't feel good about the risk."

"There's no risk. Please." She actually clasped her hands together. "Anything. Busywork. Filing. Chief, my dog is even sick of having me around so much."

Chief Dresden chuckled. "Surely you're exaggerating."

"Yeah? Get this. I was tossing his favorite fetch ball yesterday. He literally picked it up, carried it to the section of the gulch that runs behind my house and threw it in."

Dresden's gray eyebrows raised. "He didn't."

"Yes! And then he walked straight past me into the house and lay on the couch, belly-up, for three hours. He totally ignored me, even when I offered treats."

They laughed together.

"Okay, that's pretty bad."

"Tell me about it. I think he'd take *me* to the shelter if he had the chance." Erin cleared her throat, serious for a moment. She stared down at her hands in her rapidly disappearing lap. "Plus, the truth is, I need to get away from my own thoughts."

"Thoughts? About motherhood?" His expression softened. "You'll do fine, Erin. Every new mother is scared, but you'll be a natural."

"It's not so much that. Well, sort of. But, aside from that, lately, I can't stop the obsessive memories." She leveled him with a plaintive stare.

"Ah. I understand."

She knew he truly did. It wasn't just one of those things people say. Chief Dresden had been one of the volunteer firefighters on the scene twelve years earlier. They'd had meager forces and woefully inadequate equipment back then, before they'd become a paid department, but he'd dutifully responded with all the others to the infamous prom night tragedy.

They hadn't spoken of it more than twice in the entire time she'd been on the department, but he knew what Erin, Brody, Cagney and Lexy—not to mention their families and those of the kids who'd died—had gone through. He hadn't lived it, but he'd seen it. That made it easier for her to bring it up.

"So many unpleasant, scary memories, Chief, and with my hormones." She shrugged, twisting her mouth to the side. "I'm not trying to be difficult, but I need a distraction. Badly. I need my work."

He blew out a sigh, sat back in his chair and studied her, rolling ideas around in his head. "In that case, but against my better judgment, there is one thing you can do."

Her heart lifted. In truth, she was stunned. "Thank you. Really? Anything."

"The city has put together a task force to meet with the hotshot pyrotechnics company they've hired for the Fourth of July fireworks show over the lake," he said, disgust underlying his tone. "We need a representative at the meeting who truly understands the gravity of this season's fire danger."

Erin frowned. "I cannot believe they're going to proceed with fireworks. Do they want another Hayman fire situation?" she said, referring to one of the largest wildfires in Colorado history.

"I know, I know. Apparently this company, Walker Pyrotechnics, has an incredible track record for safety. The city manager's office thinks that'll be enough to keep the forest from going up in flames." He waved a hand in dismissal. "If they want to be the fire experts, I can't stop them. I answer to both the city manager and the mayor, as you know. But I want the department's views on the idea crystal clear and on record before it all goes down. I want the people of Troublesome Gulch to know that their fire department is adamantly against the show this year."

Perfect. As passionate as she was about fire prevention, this would be the ideal distraction. She leaned forward. "I'm in. What do I need to do?"

"The big powwow is day after tomorrow." He eyed her baby bulge. "Do you have a Class-A maternity uniform?"

"Yes, I borrowed Ginny Luther's. We're the same size."

He nodded once, then buzzed the secretary. "I'll have Nora get you all the data. Read it over, make some notes about all the various danger areas, every possible issue, DeLuca. Everything."

"You got it."

"And be ready to present a logical argument for canceling the event. Try your best, without alienating the rest of the city, of course."

"That, sir, will be my pleasure."

"Okay. Then, you've got yourself an assignment."

"Thank you. Again. You have no idea how much I appreciate this."

He aimed the pen at her and narrowed his gaze. "None of this is worth getting so worked up about that you stress the baby, understand?"

She laid a palm on her abdomen and smiled. "Not to worry. My baby is adamant about canceling the show, too."

The chief picked up a pen and absentmindedly tapped it on his desktop. "Your buddy, Brody

Austin, from TG Paramedics volunteered for the task force, too, so you'll have backup with your position. And he'll keep an eye on your health."

"Even better." She stood, not wanting to monopolize the busy man's day. "Those pyrotechnic guys don't stand a chance against Brody and me."

Chapter Six

Nate moved about the city conference room with purpose, reviewing his notes and setting up his PowerPoint presentation. He wasn't looking forward to meeting with the City of Troublesome Gulch Fourth of July Task Force—a mouthful, at best—but since he had no choice, he'd shown up early to amp up his A-game.

It wasn't that he had a problem answering people's safety questions—not at all. Safety had always been number one for him, hence the over-whelming demand for his business. The issue, un-fortunately, was that Troublesome Gulch was in

Colorado, and Colorado reminded him of the elusive and enigmatic Erin.

His jaw clenched.

The way she'd left still stung.

And it shouldn't. That's what made it so crazy.

It had been your classic one-night stand, nothing more. Considering that, he should be relieved there'd been no baggage to lug around afterward. The problem was, he wasn't a one-night-stand kind of guy, and even before their heart-stopping sex, something about Erin had invaded his soul, touched him, entrapped him. Hard as he tried, he couldn't get her out of his mind.

Where was she?

Was she still so sad?

Did she ever think about him?

Pathetic, but he missed her. Thought about her. Gave a damn. After one freakin' night. A blip in his history, really, but there it was. He snorted and shook his head with disdain. He really *had* watched too many romantic movies with his sisters. This was all their fault, and if he didn't rein it in, he'd find himself in the position of having his "man card" revoked permanently.

He exhaled in disgust as he tested his laptop and watched the projection screen, clicking this button and that. Computer in order, he moved on to his notes, aligning them, rereading them—

though he knew the presentation by heart. Busy-work. And he knew it.

His thoughts, of course, kept meandering back to Erin. State of the Union in his life these days. He'd even tried increasing his dating over the past several months to banish her memory, but none of the women he'd met had been half as complex or intriguing as Erin. Plus, it wasn't fair to compare every one of them to her, and that's what he found himself doing.

So he stopped dating, threw himself into his work, and avoided Colorado like a bad investment whenever he could. Since he was the boss, it wasn't difficult. He had a lot of work in the state, but he also had a posse of excellent pyrotechnicians at his disposal, and the power of delegation.

But, this year's fire season along the Rocky Mountain Front Range looked frightening at best. The notion of a fireworks show in the high country struck him as ludicrous, if not outright negligent. Were it his choice, his town, he'd cancel the show altogether. Why risk tragedy? The mayor and city manager didn't want to go that route, though.

So be it.

After he'd turned them down three separate times, the city had increased their offer to an amount he simply couldn't refuse. But he would darn well get all his safety precautions lined up well in advance, because he wasn't going to set the town on fire for the sake of stupid tradition. If that happened, he could guarantee no one would be blaming the city management. All fingers—including theirs—would be aimed directly toward Walker Pyrotechnics.

Therefore, a "task force meeting" called for the owner of Walker to attend, Colorado or not.

Painful or not.

Memories of Erin or not.

Suck it up, Nate.

The door opened, and a stream of people filed in. Nate stepped around the table to greet each of them and introduce himself. There were two men in suits, representing the mayor's office and the city manager's office, a paramedic, a cop and a secretary of some sort who fussed with the refreshments on the side table, then laid out glossy bound reports at each spot around the conference table.

He was caught up in conversation with the city manager, Walt Hennessy, when a breezy voice caught his attention.

"Sorry I'm late."

The back of his neck prickled, and his vision wavered. Rude or not, Nate's attention jerked toward the newcomer, gaping as the secretary assured her that the rest of them had just arrived, and she was just in time.

She being Erin.

His Erin.

His very *pregnant,* excruciatingly beautiful Erin, clad in—of all things—a firefighter's uniform.

This day had officially gone down the crapper.

And it also felt like the best day of his life.

Explain that.

She turned toward him and all the color drained from her face. The two of them stood frozen, staring, and the rest of the room disappeared for Nate. Oblivious, the city manager kept talking, but it became an unintelligible blah-blah-blah in Nate's ear, inconsequential. Annoying.

Erin's hands shook, he noted.

Blood roared through his skull.

The paramedic stepped in and cupped Erin's elbow, asking if she was okay, checking her pulse automatically. Was he her boyfriend? The thought tied Nate's stomach into uncomfortable knots.

"I'm fine," she said, in a testy tone, pulling her wrist away. "Sorry. But you all have to stop fussing over me like I'm some freakin' invalid."

Nate smiled tightly at the city manager. "Excuse me for a moment, sir. I apologize."

"Of course, of course," Walt Hennessy said, in his booming, blustery politician's voice.

Nate crossed the room until he and Erin stood face-to-face, so close he could smell the strawberry scent of her hair. Some insane part of him wondered if he'd simply guessed correctly when he'd bought the shampoo that night so long ago, or if she'd continued using the brand he'd purchased for more sentimental reasons.

Riiiight.

Because a woman who'd leave without so much as a kiss goodbye certainly had a sentimental bent. *Keep fooling yourself, Walker. There goes that man card.*

"Fancy meeting you here, Erin."

He watched her swallow once, then again. She pulled him toward a corner where they had some privacy. "Nate. I…I meant to—I tried to—"

"Wait a minute." The paramedic looked back and forth from the two of them, confusion on his face. "You guys already know each other?"

Erin didn't answer, just continued to gape, eyes glazed, which said everything.

Not wanting to ignore the man, Nate dropped his gaze to her very pregnant belly, let it linger, then leveled the paramedic with a wry stare. "You could say we know each other. Yes."

"Oh. *Oh,*" the paramedic said, drawing the obvious conclusions. He did a few more double takes, absorbing the new info. "Er, why didn't you—?"

Erin turned a pleading glance his way. "Brody, I…I didn't—"

"Wait." This Brody guy smiled at her. "Not now. Not here. It's okay."

"I—I promise I'll explain everything later," Erin said, before casting another sidelong glance at Nate.

The gesture sealed his suspicions.

He was going to be a father.

After quick calculations in his mind, his stomach convulsed. He was going to be a father damned *soon*. End of July.

Shaking himself back into the present, he extended his hand to the paramedic. "Nate Walker. Walker Pyrotechnics."

The medic took his hand. "Brody Austin. Pleasure to meet you." He peered curiously at Erin.

Watching, Nate knew he needed to broach the topic. "Listen," he started, "this is awkward as hell, but if you two are a couple—"

"No!" they said together.

Their vehemence took him aback.

"Brody's my best friend's husband," Erin said, in a reproachful tone, as if he should know that.

As if he'd know *anything*. "Just checking." He didn't want to acknowledge the relief that rushed through him so fast, it left his legs weak. He willed a polite, pleasant tone into his voice. "So, then. This isn't the best time for conversation, as Brody said. Are you free for coffee after the meeting? Decaf for you, obviously."

Her skin paled again. "O-of course."

The Brody guy stepped closer, chest out, chin high. "Erin, if you need Faith and me to come along—"

"No, it's okay," she told him, with a reassuring smile. "It's nothing like…whatever you're thinking. Really. Let's just drop it for now and get this meeting underway. Okay?"

Meeting? What meeting?

The only fireworks for Nate right now were those exploding in his brain. So much for bringing his A-game during this all-important presentation.

Chapter Seven

The meeting passed in a blur of rote presentation mixed with swirling unanswerable questions and pure blinding shock. An irrational part of him resented having been put in that position, even though he logically knew neither he nor Erin would've planned it that way. She didn't know he was Walker Pyrotechnics any more than he'd known she was a Troublesome Gulch firefighter. Still, during the meeting, he hadn't treated her like the bad guy simply because of her choice of profession. It would've been nice if she'd extended him the same courtesy.

In any case, Nate left the city building feeling as though he'd at least conveyed his main bullet points.

Then again, who cared?

An unfamiliar glut of emotions crested and crashed inside him. Joy. Fear. Anger. Excitement.

He was going to be a father. A *father.*

And a damn sight better father than his ever was, too, regardless of the fact that this whole thing was so utterly unexpected. He'd always imagined he'd have a wife long before the father issue arose, but apparently fate had dealt him a different hand. Which was fine.

Still, he felt woefully unprepared. Erin'd had about seven months to get used to the idea while he was left with the cram course.

When the meeting room had cleared, they'd agreed to meet at the Pinecone Diner rather than driving together. Erin wanted to change out of her uniform—or at least that was her excuse. Naturally, he arrived first. He took a table in the rear of the place and sat, back to the wall, waiting. Thinking. Fuming.

Truth be told, the more he went over the whole convoluted situation in his mind, the more wicked-pissed he became. He'd bet more steam rose off him than off his freshly poured mug of coffee, which he gripped with angry hands.

Pregnancy aside, he couldn't get past the fact

that she'd seemed downright hostile during the task force meeting. Why? What had he done to deserve that? First of all, had she been listening to him at all instead of tossing him eye daggers the whole time, she would know that he basically agreed with her stance about the fireworks show, and was doing his best to make it safe. She'd also realize that she hadn't hired him. He couldn't just change things based on her opinion, as much as he'd like to.

Even more aggravating, *she* was the one who'd run out of the hotel room without so much as a courtesy phone number on her quickly scrawled note. Had she not, they might know more about each other at this point. He was blameless in both situations.

Straight up, she should've told him about the baby. Somehow. This was the information age, after all.

At the very least, she shouldn't have lied about her ability to conceive. He'd been honest that night. Open. He'd tried to help her, to comfort her, and— stupid him—he'd truly thought they'd connected on more than a sexual level. How hard would it have been for her to leave a contact phone number instead of skulking out of that hotel room like a criminal? An e-mail address at the very least? Had he given her any red flag indications whatsoever that he harbored stalker tendencies? No way.

Then again, he'd known the game going in. This slap in the face was exactly the kind of treatment a man got when he played savior in a dive bar.

He should've expected it.

His fists clenched. Absurd as it sounded, he just *hadn't* expected the stereotypical ending from the Erin he thought he'd begun to know that night. He'd hoped for better from her. That was the biggest shame in the whole, tangled fiasco.

The bell over the door jingled, and there she stood.

His breath caught.

She was a thousand times more beautiful carrying his child than she'd been that night. Ripe, robust, radiant. Damn it, despite it all, he couldn't hold back his elation at seeing her again, and that weakness irked him. She stopped, scanning the crowd, waving to a few of the people she knew.

In a small town like this, she surely knew everyone. He didn't envy her the task she'd probably faced of explaining how she wound up pregnant when she didn't even have a boyfriend.

But he'd save his sympathy. After how she'd treated him, she didn't deserve it.

When she saw him, her expression registered immediate distress, which he hated. They both knew this was going to suck, but he'd always hoped she would look at him with a very different expression in her eyes if they ever met again.

She raised her hand nervously, and headed his way. It was mid-June, warm for the high country. She wore some sort of billowy white top and jeans. Flip-flops. As she approached, it occurred to him that she wasn't very large for being seven months along. From behind, you wouldn't even know she was pregnant.

A sickening feeling bloomed inside his chest.

Maybe this wasn't his baby after all.

The thought didn't comfort him as one might expect it would.

"Hi," she said, as she slid into the booth. "Have you been waiting long?"

"Only about seven months," he said.

She froze from the ice in his tone, color rising into her cheeks as though windburned. "Nate, God, I—"

"Hey, Erin, honey," said the waitress, sidling up at precisely the worst time ever. "It's good to see you out and about. You look just adorable—you're one of *those* pregnant women, lucky you. Lordy, I was an absolute cow with my kids," she added wistfully, before shaking off the memory. "Anyway, how much longer?"

Erin glanced furtively toward Nate. He could read her dismay at the line of conversation, but what could she do?

Nate sat back, languidly raising an eyebrow,

daring her to answer. Hell, at this point, he wanted to know, too. He tried for a calm demeanor, but beneath the table, his fists clenched.

"Ah, just about eight weeks. Thanks."

His insides shook with relief. Confirmed: his kid. She must just be one of those women who carried small, probably due to her amazing physical condition.

"You have everything all ready?"

She cleared her throat. "Almost."

"Well, we can't wait to meet him or her." The clueless waitress smiled his way before turning back toward Erin. "I already served your friend here. But can I get you something to drink?"

"Just water. Oh, and I guess I'll have a glass of skim milk, too."

"Gotta feed that little one," the waitress sang, as she turned and headed off.

"Should you really do the skim thing?"

She blew out a breath of exasperation. "Yes. I can't gain a lot of weight. Doctor's orders. And please don't start watchdogging my every move. I get enough of that from everyone around here."

Silence descended.

"Nice that the whole world knows everything about you and the pregnancy except the baby's father," he said.

She flinched. "I didn't know your last name,"

she said, her tone low and laced tight with regret. "I looked for you. I swear. On Google and I called the hotel…but all I had was Nate."

"I stay there all the time," he said.

"Yes, and their privacy policies don't include giving out your information to strange women, which I suppose you should be grateful for. It might've made things easier had I known you were a fire setter," she snapped.

He sighed. Again with the hostility. He harnessed flame for entertainment purposes. She was a firefighter. He got the polarity issue. But, her animosity toward his chosen profession was over-the-top and unwarranted, and he was sick of avoiding the real cause. "I'm not a fire setter. I'm a pyrotechnics engineer, and a damned good one. If you'll recall, you didn't want to know anything about me that night or I would've gladly told you. Don't twist this around and act like I hid something from *you*."

She had the decency to look chagrined. "Sorry."

He scowled. "Why did you tell me you couldn't get pregnant in the first place? Why the lie? Just to save you the trip to the donor clinic?"

"No! It wasn't a lie," she said, her tone brittle. She glanced around, lowered it again. "I wasn't trying to rope some unassuming guy into getting me pregnant, okay? No matter what you think.

Please, I realize you don't owe me any favors, but can we agree to keep our voices down?"

She pressed shaky fingers to the middle of her forehead. Long fingers. Short, bare nails.

Sexy.

"This is a small town. Everyone knows everyone, and I don't want us or our baby to be fodder for the Gulch gossip mill."

He inclined his head. "That's reasonable." Frankly, he didn't want strangers here knowing his business, either.

She reached across the table and touched his hand with those warm, sexy fingers, but pulled back almost immediately. "I *honestly* believed I couldn't conceive. It wasn't a lie. This pregnancy was as much a surprise to me as it is to you."

He scoffed.

"It was. And when I found out, the first thing I wanted was to tell you. I've agonized over it for the past five months."

"Really," he said, his tone dubious.

"Yes, and I can only thank God you ended up here now. Belated, but here it is." She spread her arms wide. "You're going to be a father. Okay? I'm sorry you couldn't be here for the morning sickness, the leg cramps and the smothering inquiries from my friends and family, but trust me when I say you really didn't miss much excitement."

"Your perspective."

Her chin quivered. "What else was I supposed to do, Nate? What? Tell me."

He blew out a sigh of resignation. They couldn't change the past, and he had to take her at her word. "Okay, we made a lot of mistakes from the start. Both of us. I guess my bottom line is, you shouldn't have left without saying goodbye. I deserved more."

Misery molded her expression. "I *know.*"

"Great. You know. So, what now?" he asked, more roughly than he'd intended.

She bristled. "Now? Nothing." Her tough shell slammed shut around her. "I'm not planning on milking you for financial support, if that's what you're stressing about."

"Financial support?" He could swear his ears burst into flames with the force of his rage. "Is that what you think I'm concerned about?"

She blinked, uncertain and off-kilter from his quick flash of anger. "Well, what else? It was—" she lowered to a whisper "—a one-night stand. I don't expect you to go down on one knee and pledge your life to me."

"Which I have no intention of doing," he hissed, regretting it only slightly when he saw the hurt cloud her expression. "But, regardless of our relationship, or the lack thereof, I intend to be a part of my child's life. I have that right."

Fear rolled off of her like storm clouds over the mountain range, and she rested a protective hand on her belly. "If you try to take my child—"

"Back up one damn minute," He splayed a palm on his chest. "I'm angry right now, yes. I have every right to be. Even you can't deny that."

Standoff.

"Okay, you're right." She sagged. "Sorry."

"Please, try to see past it all. Remember me? Nate? I'm the good guy—your words, not mine. The one you said my mom should be proud of. Does any of that ring a bell?"

She bit the corner of her bottom lip.

"If you honestly think I would take my baby away from his mother, then we connected even less than I imagined. In fact, we didn't connect at all, and considering a child resulted from such a complete disconnect, that's a damned disgrace."

She forced out a breath and pushed all ten fingers into the front of her hair. "No, that's not it. We did connect, Nate."

His heart jumped.

"I—I just don't know what to think. I'm flustered and I'm scared. I never thought I'd see you again. I never thought I'd get pregnant in the first place. And then you're here in Troublesome Gulch. Suddenly."

"Surprise," he said, unable to keep the sarcasm out of his tone.

She ignored it. "No one knows anything about you, not even my closest friends. This is all just so—"

The waitress returned with her beverages, and they both went silent. The woman seemed to sense the seriousness of their conversation, because she didn't indulge in any more chatter. Thank God. When she walked away, Erin finished with, "—so complicated."

Nate leaned forward, winding both hands around his thick, ceramic coffee mug. "What's complicated about it? Introduce me to your friends any way you need to." He flicked his hand to the side. "That part, I don't care about. Next step, you give birth to our child. We share custody. Problem solved." He paused, but she didn't comment. "We're supposedly friends, right? At least, I thought so." He squinted off into the distance. "Then again, there was that note."

"*Enough* with the note already," she said, her tone exasperated. "I've apologized. How many more times can I say I'm sorry?" She ignored the friend part altogether. "Your solution sounds pat and perfect, but the custody arrangement is impossible. I'm not sending my baby off to Las Vegas a couple times a month. Who can afford that?"

"*Our* baby. And no one's suggesting twice monthly interstate flight. Do I look like an idiot to you?"

She lifted her chin, but her bottom lip tremored. "My career is here, and so are my friends and family. I can't start over in Las Vegas. I don't even want to."

"Not a problem, because I own my company and work all over the country." He shrugged. "Where I'm headquartered means nothing to my clients."

She blinked at him. Twice. "What are you saying?"

"I'm saying, I'll move to Troublesome Gulch. Now. Before my child is born."

She gasped.

He held up a hand. "Listen, you can hate me, avoid me, deny you ever begged me to make love to you, even though we both know you did."

Her face bloomed crimson; she cut away her glance.

"Blame the whole fiasco on me if you have to. Whatever gets you through the day. But one thing I can guarantee you, Erin, is that my child will not grow up without a father. That is a nonnegotiable point."

All around them, diner business proceeded as usual while they sat cloaked in weighty, silent distress. The waitresses called orders out to the cooks, diners conversed. Silverware clinked against plates and bowls. Laughter.

"I don't hate you," she said softly. "Not one single bit."

That admission surprised him. He took a moment to school his tone into ambivalence. "Well, there's a bit of good news for once."

"And I'd never blame the whole thing on you. You should give me a little credit, too." She studied him from beneath her long, dark lashes. "But I know I don't deserve your credit, and I'd understand if *you* hated *me*."

He melted a bit, in spite of his ire. "No such luck. You're carrying our baby, remember? I couldn't hate you if I tried."

The tension in her face eased. "I'm…I'm glad. Really. And, for the last time—I hope—" she eyed him pointedly "—I'm sorry for leaving the infamous note. I was wrong. Unfair. But, you witnessed my state of mind more than anyone that night. I didn't know how to handle—" she blew out a breath "—look, I can't change it. You have no idea how many times I've wished I could. But, I'll make it up to you. As a friend. And we *are* friends. Just tell me how. Please."

He sipped his coffee, watching her over the rim. After he'd swallowed, he set the mug back down. "Maybe, as *friends* and for the sake of our baby, we can call a truce, leave the past where it belongs."

"Deal. Thank goodness."

"And…" He toyed with the rim of his coffee mug,

shook his head, unsure. Maybe this was too much to ask at this tenuous juncture in their relationship.

"And?"

Hell, what did he have to lose? "Can you help me find a place to live?"

She worried her fingers together, considering. "That's a reasonable request. But I have one equally reasonable condition."

"Name it."

"You didn't ask to be a father, Nate. I have no expectations of you." She swallowed. Twice. "If there is any chance whatsoever that you're going to disappear in a few years, I'd rather you just did it now. Before the baby gets attached to you. Please," she asked, in a whisper. "I don't want our baby heartbroken."

Emotions from the past swamped him. He leaned in. "Erin, do you remember what I told you about my family that night?"

Bafflement showed on her face. "Um, it was you, your mom and three sisters, your dad wasn't involv—oh."

"Yeah. *Oh.*" He let that sink in. "I do remember my dad, for the record. I remember waiting on the front porch for his promised visits, excited, eager, my Spider-Man duffel bag packed. I remember my mom gently pulling me inside the house as the sun went down, because the bastard never showed.

I remember crying myself to sleep, inconsolable. Those are the memories of my father."

"I'm sorry."

He shrugged. "The point is, I would never put my child in the position my father put me and my sisters into. Never. I may not have asked to be a dad, but strange as it seems, I want this baby."

"I do, too," she said, in a near whisper.

"I want to be a parent to him. Or her. A real parent, not someone to wait for on the porch. End of story."

She cocked her head. "Your word of honor?"

"Absolutely."

After a deep breath, she said, "In that case, I probably know of a place you can buy immediately. If it fits your needs, that is."

He stilled, waiting.

"You met my friend Brody at the meeting?"

"Yes."

"His wife, Faith, is my best friend, and she moved into his house when they married but hasn't sold her condo yet." She shrugged. "It's small— one bedroom—but in a great area downtown, and partially furnished with the stuff that couldn't fit at Brody's. Plus, she really needs to sell. She's pregnant, too. Due in September. And they have a teenage foster son who'll be off to college before they know it."

He nodded once. "Perfect. Sign me up."

Her brows arched. "Really? You haven't even seen the condo."

"Doesn't matter. A place to live, no waiting, help out your friends. It's a win-win."

She gave him an angelic smile that warmed his soul more than it probably should've, considering.

"Faith will be thrilled. It's a nice place, Nate. I promise."

"What matters is that I'll be here."

Erin grew distant, twirled her spoon absentmindedly against the table.

He hated to see her sad. It reminded him of that night. "Why so pensive? Seems like we've made some progress here."

She half shrugged. "I don't know." She bit her bottom lip. "You're really going to uproot your life?"

"What would you do in my place?"

A line of worry bisected her forehead. "But what about your family? Your mom and sisters?" Her eyes widened, and she reached up to cover her mouth. "Oh no. Boomer and Thug."

He frowned. "What about them?"

The ache of remorse weighed down her words. "Pets aren't allowed in Faith's condo building, Nate. They're your family. I know how important they are to you."

True pain lanced through him, but he fought it

off. Somehow, some way, it would all work out. "My child is my family, too."

She thought for a moment, moistening her lips with a nervous flick of her tongue. "Would it be okay if Boomer and Thug stayed at my house? I'm sure Finn would love them, though we'd have to test him with the bunny."

"That's okay with you?"

"It's the least I can do. Plus, who knows? Maybe Faith's condo can be a stepping stone until you find something more suitable. At least it'll get you here now. They'll probably let you move in before the closing."

"It's a solution at least. Thanks. As for Mom and the girls, I have regular work in Las Vegas. The way I travel, I'll see them as much as I do now. More, because I'll stay at their houses when I'm there, and they'll actually feed me. And, of course, they'll want to come here often and see the baby once he or she is born." He hesitated, softened his tone. "Meet you."

She gulped. He could see the whole spiderweb of extended family layering on more complications in her mind. This was why no-strings sex was a big fat myth.

"What are you going to tell them?"

"No clue. I'm still reeling myself."

"I'm so sorry, Nate. You were good to me, and

I never intended to put you in this awkward position with your family. With your *life*. You deserve...the total package. True love, marriage, family." She twisted her mouth to the side. "Instead, you're stuck with me and a baby you never wanted."

Strangely, despite the emotional wood chipper he'd been thrust through today, he wasn't sorry. In a zillion scattered pieces, flailing for emotional purchase, but certainly not sorry. He reached out and covered her hand with his, ventured an encouraging, if winsome, smile. "We've had a bit of a rough start, but everything will be fine. You'll see. We're both adults, and these are modern times. Unmarried parents? Not such a big deal."

"No," she murmured.

"One thing we're both committed to is making sure our baby knows he or she is loved and wanted. Right?"

"Absolutely."

He shrugged, pulled his hand back. "Then we're on the same page. The only page that counts." He paused, searched her eyes. "Be in the moment, right?"

Chapter Eight

Erin's regular Friday lunch date with Faith rolled around a few days after Nate exploded back into her life like a bottle rocket. Everything was in fast-forward mode. He was scheduled to move in to Faith's old condo that weekend, as a renter until they could close the sale. And she wanted to lay out the whole sordid tale for her friends before he was officially a part of their lives. So, she invited Brody, Cagney and Lexy along, with Faith's encouragement.

Once they'd ordered and eaten, she sucked it up and spilled the whole story.

Wasn't easy, either, to say the least.

As she neared the end of the explanation, her paper napkin lay in tatters on her lap, and her friends watched her with concern etched into their sober expressions. "The Millstone apartment fire just really brought it all back for me, I don't know. No other fire has been like that. I think it was Suzette—"

"Who is recovering nicely," Brody said, "as is her beautiful, healthy baby girl."

She bestowed a quick half smile. "I'm glad. But that night, all I knew was she'd lost her husband. I was stupid, out of control." She shrugged. "Nate was there, I was there. Just us in a hotel room, and…I started to think about Brody."

"Yeah—" he puffed his chest out playfully "—I have that effect on women." He winked at her.

Faith punched him in the arm.

Erin forged ahead, ignoring his total guyness. "I mean, I've always claimed that I'd worked through what happened to us on prom night, but it's not true. I've just honed the art of putting up a perfect front."

"Me, too," Cagney said.

"Me, three," Lexy added.

Erin regarded them sadly. "The truth is, my life had been at a standstill since I lost Kev. And the baby. The first baby. Brody had returned to the Gulch and done such a good job of working through his issues."

He curled Faith against his side. "Thanks to my lovely pregnant wife and the best in-laws a man could have."

She leaned up and kissed him on the chin.

Erin and the others smiled. "You two. Anyway, in my desperate and probably not-so-rational analysis of the situation, I concluded that Brody had gotten on with his life because he'd taken one difficult step—moving back to the Gulch, no matter how terrifying."

He leaned his head side to side. "Pretty much true."

"See? So, I decided to take *my* one difficult and terrifying step. With Nate." Heat suffused her whole body, and she rested a hand on her belly. She didn't even want to know how red-faced she was. "I guess I don't have to tell you what that step entailed."

"No, we get it," Faith said.

"And who knew," she tossed off, her tone wry. "All that crap they pounded into our brains during high school health class was dead-on. You truly can get pregnant from just once."

"Aw, honey. No one blames you," Lexy said. Her hair was red this month, an ultramodern cut, always the little siren. "None of us have any room to judge. You're a grown woman. Besides, I've seen Nate Walker at the city building. That man is fine, fine, fine."

Erin cleared her throat, feeling itchy inside her clothing. "That was part of it, sure. He was the first guy since Kev to actually make me think...along those lines." She choked back a wave of embarrassment. "But the night didn't start that way, honestly. I was a mess, and he was only trying to help. He's such a nice, genuine guy."

"No one's implying he seduced you or took advantage of you in your time of weakness, if that's what this is all about," Cagney said.

Erin nodded. "It is. Part of it. I'd been so scared for so long. But, I could never have done that with anyone who wasn't..."

Nate, she thought, with a lightning bolt of shock. She couldn't have made love with any other man. That sudden insight shook her to her core.

"I'd say he's more than just nice," Cagney interjected, her sandy blond hair in its neat, workday French braid, though strands of it had wisped their way out to frame her delicate features. She'd taken a lunch break in order to join them, still wearing her TG Police uniform. "I mean, he's uprooting to a whole new state just to be an involved father." She shook her head in amazement. "Not a lot of guys would go that far."

"I approve," Faith said, raising a hand.

Brody nodded. "Stand-up man, that Nate."

"You are my closest friends," Erin said. She

looked at each of them in turn. "I really wanted to tell you this, excruciating as it was, well, first, because of the blame issue. I didn't want you to feel like you had to take sides."

"We don't," Faith said. "Truly."

"Good." Erin readjusted in her chair. "But I also wanted to have this talk because I hope…" She pulled her bottom lip in between her teeth, feeling an unexpected surge of protectiveness toward Nate.

"Hope what, Er?" Cagney urged.

"I guess…that each of you will find a way to welcome Nate into the fold, too. I mean—" she held up her palms "—he and I are not a couple. Despite the baby. After the way I left things, trust me, that could never happen."

"Never say never," Lexy sang, studying her manicure.

Erin couldn't even address that notion. "But, after all he's sacrificing, I want him to have friends here, and you're the best people I know. You have to believe none of this was his fault."

"It wasn't yours, either. You were in a bad place, and you did what you had to do. But you have great instincts," Cagney said. "If you welcome him, we'll welcome him."

A chorus of agreements went around the table.

"That said," Cagney added, placing her palms on the tabletop, "I, unfortunately, have to get back to the old day-in, day-out grind." She pulled a face. "But, if you want him to take over as your birth coach, all you need to do is tell me. I'll understand."

Erin slashed her hands through the air. "No way. You are my birth coach. Period."

"Well…okay," her quietly stoic friend said, unsure. "I'm absolutely here for you. But, if I may ask, what does Nate think about that?"

Erin shrugged.

"Erin?" Cagney pressed.

"It, uh, hasn't come up."

Lexy lowered her chin. "You're due in less than eight weeks. He's the father. It *needs* to come up."

"I know, I know. And when it does, I'll deal with it. Promise. No more running. But I need Cagney with me in the delivery room. And, before I confront anything about the actual birth, I need to get past the fact that he's moving here. Tomorrow. Oh, my God." She waved a hand in front of her face, breathing rapidly.

Lexy maneuvered her wheelchair closer to Erin and leaned forward to hug her. "We love you, you big dork. We're just trying to help. Stop depriving your fetus of oxygen."

"I'm trying."

"No one cares that your pregnancy is the result of a one-night stand. The baby has seemed to make you happier, and I, for one, just want you to be happy." The tiny little firebrand glanced around at the table of friends. "I want you all to be happy, since any unhappiness you might feel, as we know, is my fault."

"No, it isn't, Lex. Let it go, already," Cagney said, scraping back her chair to stand. "We make our own joy, we make our own sorrow."

Lexy brushed her off. She'd always blamed herself for the radical changes in their lives, discounting the fact that her change—at least physically—was the most extreme by far.

Cagney leaned down to kiss Erin on the cheek. "I've really got to go. It's all good, girlfriend. Nate's a good guy. Your baby's healthy. Your friends love you and so does your family. So, don't worry. It'll all work out somehow." She winked at the others and left the restaurant.

The remaining friends moved their chairs in closer.

"Speaking of tomorrow, Jason and I still plan on helping Nate move in, whenever he rolls into town," Brody said. "Any idea when?"

"None. Sorry."

"Does he have my numbers?"

"Yes."

"I'll help, too," Faith said.

"Like hell you will," her husband said, giving her a dark glare. He aimed a similar one at Erin.

"If I catch either of you lifting or moving anything, I'll have Cagney handcuff you inside her car for the duration."

"Well, we want to *be* there," Faith said. "We're pregnant, not helpless, for God's sake. This isn't 1812. We can at least provide refreshments."

"Fine. You can be there." He pointed at Erin. "Keep my wife a minimum of ten feet away from the coffeemaker. She still can't manage to brew a pot of joe that isn't pure, choking poison."

"Deal."

Faith scrunched her nose at Erin. "Traitor."

Erin shrugged in apology. "Your coffee sucks, Pip. We can't lie, because we love you."

Lexy laughed.

Brody raised his brows at Faith. "And you, keep Erin from working. We all know how she is. If she so much as unpacks one pillowcase, I will rat her out to Dr. Kipfer and the fire chief, with not an iota of guilt."

"Geez, you play dirty, Austin," Erin said, amused by his overprotectiveness. She had to admit, it felt good to be cared for. Sometimes. She sipped her lemonade, a huge burden lifted from her shoulders.

"Damn right I do." He grinned, then turned to Lexy. "And your task, little one, is to keep the city running smoothly tomorrow while the *finest* of TG's finest are busy, okay?"

She rolled her big, green eyes. "Duh, Brody. Don't I always?"

"That, you do."

"I may not have made it to my coronation ceremony on prom night, but never forget, I will always be the queen of Troublesome Gulch." She laughed. "Wow, I'm a legend in my own mind."

The moving in went smoothly enough, though the day ran painfully long. It seemed as if Nate hadn't brought much. Erin didn't know if that was because he lived simply due to all his traveling, or because the whole situation really was temporary to him, despite what he'd claimed. Worry set her on edge regardless.

That, and raging hormones.

She hated the freakin' things.

PMS had nothin' on pregnancy.

When they'd finished situating all of Nate's stuff, Jason, Brody's and Faith's foster son, sat on the floor playing with Boomer and Thug, and Brody and Nate engaged in some mind-numbing, irrelevant sports prattle, getting along fine, no worries whatsoever—damned irritating males. Erin and Faith hovered on the outskirts tentatively. Like…okay, guys, what next? Frankly, going home seemed like a grand idea.

Erin's jaw clenched. She desperately yearned

for some alone time and a much-needed nap. Plus, she could tell by her friend's pinched expression that Faith's back hurt, an issue she'd suffered from since her first trimester.

Faith wouldn't readily admit to her pain, though. She was too nice for her own good. One palm pressed to her lower back, she smiled stiffly at the guys. "So, we're done. That wasn't too awful," she lied, in a pathetic attempt at hint dropping.

Erin snorted, not caring if she sounded unladylike.

Brody glanced at Faith. "How about we all head over to our house for dinner, babe? Nate's pantry isn't stocked yet, and a home-cooked meal sure would be a great welcome tonight."

Inside, Erin groaned. Brody and his big mouth. Friend or not, she so wanted to smack the guy. God knows, he probably wasn't offering to whip up a welcome meal, and she darn well wasn't going to stand by and watch Faith slaving away. "Actually, we might as well have dinner at my house," she said, throwing a subtle stink-eye Brody's way.

"You don't have to cook for me." Nate smiled at her. "Thanks, but restaurant food is a staple in my life. Besides, I'm sure both you and Faith are tired."

She appreciated his perceptiveness about their exhaustion, as Brody didn't seem to have clue number one. However, she still felt unduly peeved that Nate had considered, even for a moment, the notion that she might stand before a hot stove on his behalf. Or anyone's, for that matter.

Nearly eight months pregnant in *summer*—hello!

"Oh, trust me, I'm not cooking. We can order out. But we do need to get Boomer and Thug settled. I wouldn't mind having everyone there in case Finn suddenly decides Thug looks like dinner instead of a new furry pal."

Jason's head whipped up, one hand protectively stroking Thug's back. "Dude, that's cold. Ain't no way you should let Finn eat this rabbit. He rocks, 'specially his name."

"Well, I wouldn't *let* him—"

"Don't call Erin 'dude,' Jase," Faith interrupted, sounding as though she were balanced, tiptoe, on her last nerve. "It's disrespectful. I've told you that a million times."

Jason had always hated disappointing Faith. He ducked his reddened face. "My bad. Ms. DeLuca."

"Ugh," Erin said, rolling her eyes. "You can't call me *that,* either. It makes me feel ancient. And *fat.*"

"Uh, fat?" Jason cast a confused, pleading glance toward Brody.

"Don't worry, buddy." He sent the teenager a reassuring wink. "Pregnant women are known to be virtually incomprehensible."

"Shut up!" Erin and Faith said, in stereo.

"My God, Brody!" Faith's eyes flashed. She

planted her fists on her hips. "*That's* what you want to teach him about women? That we're irrational because we're carrying *your* children?"

Awkwardness descended as a WWE match between Venus and Mars unexpectedly ensued. It might be two against three, but the men were hormonally outclassed, in a pro ball versus Little League sort of way.

"Ah…I'm sorry?" Brody ventured.

"Is that a statement or a question?" Faith asked.

"I have a better idea," Nate interjected, in as light a tone as it seemed he could manage while venturing into the danger zone. He smoothed his palms together a couple times. "Boomer and Thug are fine here tonight. They've always been quiet. No one will know the difference. Why don't you ladies take the evening off. Relax in a testosterone-free environment."

"Sounds like bliss," Erin said.

"More like nirvana," said Faith, with a sigh.

"Or heaven," said Erin.

"Then, it's settled. Brody, Jason and I will head off for some food and get out of your way." He glanced toward Brody, who eagerly nodded.

"Don't forget, I'm supposed to spend the night with Gramps," Jason said, referring to old Mr. Norwood, who used to own Brody and Faith's A-frame and had become an integral part of their little patchwork family. "He scored the newest Xbox game, so I have to kick his butt at it a few times before he works on his skills. Dude has way too much time to practice. It's not fair."

"Perfect," Brody said, grabbing the escape rope from the hormone hell pit he'd unwittingly fallen into. He tried to match his tone to Nate's, but sounded a bit too saccharine, as though carefully addressing homicidal maniacs. It didn't help his case.

"Babe, we'll drive you and Erin home, drop Jase at Herman's and then Nate and I will make ourselves scarce. Sound good?"

"Whatever," Faith snapped.

"Don't bother. I can drive Faith home," Erin said, holding up one palm as Brody opened his mouth to comment. "And if either one of you even starts to say that I shouldn't be driving, I can't be held responsible for my actions. You'd better just get out while you can."

Eyes round, Jason shot to his feet and backed away from the women. Brody clamped a hand on his shoulder. "Son, a wise man simply listens to a pregnant woman and does what she says—"

"Preferably without *comment*," Faith added, pointedly. She ground her fist into her back. "God, I need a heating pad. And a margarita, but ha ha, joke's on me, right?"

Concern furrowed Brody's forehead. "Does your back hurt, babe?"

"Of course her back hurts. She's carrying twenty-five extra pounds up-front, for God's sake," Erin barked, pointing toward the front door. "Stop asking idiotic questions, Austin. Go!"

All three men scurried off.

"We'll lock up if that's okay, Nate," Faith called after them. "Erin can give you the spare set of keys tomorrow or whenever."

He held up both hands in acquiescence, saying nothing. Smart man. When the guys closed the door behind them, as quietly as possible, Faith and Erin exhaled simultaneous sighs of relief and exasperation. Then, unexpectedly, they looked at each other and burst out laughing. Hard.

"I hate men," Faith said, when the hysteria had subsided. She wiped tears from her eyes.

"I hear you. Such an annoying breed of human."

"And clueless? Geez."

"Completely."

"I never realized just *how* clueless until I got pregnant. 'Babe, why don't we all have dinner over at our house,'" Faith said, mimicking her husband's voice. She bugged her eyes at Erin. "What was *that*?"

"That was Brody being Brody. You'd usually melt at how sweet he was being."

"Sweet, schmeet. I wonder if I have a cheese-cake in the freezer?"

Erin smoothed a palm over her belly. "Ready to go? I'm exhausted. The baby's been kicking the crap out of me all day, and I'm *so* over it. I'm hoping a bath will zen him out."

Faith palmed the extra set of keys from the coffee table. "More than ready. I want a cup of tea, a heating pad and silence. And, so help me God, there'd better not be one single sock or pair of boxer briefs on my damn floor, or those guys are in for it."

That sent them into hysterics again, until they were both crossing their legs and holding their bellies. Once they'd pulled themselves together, they staggered side by side toward the door. Erin hugged Faith around the shoulders. "It's so comforting to go through this insanity with someone who really gets it."

"I know." Faith chuckled, then blew out a sigh. "Although even *I* don't get it sometimes. I've got to snap out of it. That whole exchange with Brody felt like an out-of-body experience."

"Yeah, I kept waiting for your head to spin around," Erin said, in a wry tone.

Faith grimaced. "I suppose we were a little hard on them, you know?"

"Eh, screw it." Erin flicked her fingers to the

side. "They're probably going to devour big plates of greasy Mexican food—"

"And *my* margarita," Faith said.

"Like they possess such good taste. Please. They'll drink beers."

"True."

"And then they'll shoot a few games of pool as if they have no cares in the world. All while we sit at home, cranky and contemplating our swollen ankles and aching backs."

"Good point. Jerks." She hesitated, then sighed again, ever the romantic. "Still, I'm madly in love with Brody, and despite his forays into the supremely annoying, he's so good to me."

Erin thought of Nate. "I know what you mean."

Faith did a double take.

"What?" Erin asked.

A smug smile overtook Faith's face.

"What?"

"I didn't say a word."

Erin started shaking her head before she even uttered a sound. "Oh, no. Don't go there. I *so* did not mean that I felt the same way about Nate. Don't even think you're reading between my lines."

"Uh-huh."

"You and Brody are *married,*" Erin enunciated, as they opened the front door. "Nate and I don't even know each other."

"Whatever you say." Faith paused, still looking smug. "But, you must admit, he *is* really sweet. Sure seems like a guy worth getting to know."

"Whatever you say," Erin echoed, with sarcasm in her tone, although she secretly agreed. But, she'd never cop to it, no matter how much she wished they could just start over. After the way she'd treated him, no chance she would set herself up for more heartbreak.

She glanced back at Boomer and Thug, nestled together on the dog bed. Boomer thumped his tail against the floor and Thug twitched his long whiskers, which made her smile. They were male, true enough, but at least they were neutered.

"Have fun in your new temporary house, fuzzy guys. See you tomorrow."

Chapter Nine

They'd consumed mass quantities of excellent Mexican food and had each ordered a second beer delivered to the pool table they'd laid their quarters on earlier. It felt good to be out of the female crosshairs, enjoying uncomplicated male companionship for u while.

Nate would always love Vegas, because it was home. But he had to admit, he'd felt really welcomed since his move to Troublesome Gulch. So far, the small town atmosphere suited him.

He knew he had Erin to thank for that.

Not that he had a clue how to thank her.

Brody aimed his pool cue. "Eight ball, side pocket." He leaned down for the shot, knocked it in cleanly.

"Good game." Nate offered a hand, which Brody shook.

"Another?"

Nate shrugged. "Why not? First night in a new place is always uncomfortable, and I'm thinking you'd be wise to avoid going home for a while yet."

Brody whistled through his teeth as he racked the balls. "This pregnancy thing. Man, it's rough. My Faith was a perky, cheery little angel before it all hit. Now, some days, all Jason and I can do is walk lightly and dodge the direct shots."

Nate laughed. "I'm just grateful to finally be a part of it, mood swings and all."

"Oh, I am, too. But, it's nice to have another guy to commiserate with." Brody chalked his cue, then lifted his chin. "Go ahead and break."

Nate lined up his shot.

Brody sniffed. "You know Erin would've told you sooner had she been able."

Nate raised an eyebrow. "You think?"

"I've known the girl since high school, basically, although I've only gotten to know her really well in the past year. She's solid."

Nate broke hard, sinking two stripes. He moved around the table looking for a new angle, but his mind was on the lines of communication about Erin that Brody had opened up. Nate had so many questions. He called his shot, missed, then stepped back toward the row of bar stools to give Brody room for his turn. After a long pull on his Corona, Nate braved it. "Can I ask you a question about her?"

Brody, circling and scrutinizing the table, didn't even glance up. "About Erin? Sure."

"Why was she so hostile toward me during the task force meeting? Couldn't she tell I was more on her side than on the city manager's?"

"It wasn't you." Brody leaned down, lined up and knocked in a solid so crisply, he left the cue ball spinning in place at the mouth of the pocket. "I just don't know that she can be objective about that stuff, buddy. Ever since she was burned so badly in our prom night accident, she's pretty against recreational fire of any kind. It's understandable."

Shock riddled through Nate. His fingers tingled. "Erin was burned? Where?"

Brody froze, dismay moving over his expression. "Damn it. I assumed you knew. You two had… I mean, she's…" He pantomimed a big round belly.

Nate put it together. "Her abdomen is burned?" He clenched his fists, lambasting himself silently. That explained the long period of celibacy, the unwillingness to remove her shirt when they made love. It could even explain her belief that she wouldn't be able to conceive in the first place.

It explained *a lot*.

God, he wished he could gather her into his arms right then, apologize, reassure her that everything would be okay. Not that she'd want his comfort. Brody still hadn't answered.

"Is that it?" he pressed. "Her abdomen?"

He could see Brody silently chastising himself for the breach of trust, but it was too late now. "She was in that burn treatment center for months, I guess. I've never seen the scars, of course, but Faith says they're extensive. You, uh, you didn't notice them yourself?"

"Well—"

"Never mind." Brody held up a hand. "I don't need intimate details. You have to know, I didn't intend to spill any secrets Erin didn't want spilled. I'm feeling a bit guilty."

Nate sank onto a bar stool. "I'm feeling stunned myself. She didn't say anything. To answer your question, no, I didn't see any scars."

Brody studied him quizzically.

"Long story for another night and many more beers. I mean, she said she had an injury, which is why she thought she couldn't conceive, but—" He shrugged.

Brody leaned on his pool cue, seeming to contemplate the situation. Finally, he nodded his head once, mouth in a grim line. "Listen. This isn't my story to tell—"

"Of course. I understand. Shouldn't have asked."

"Wait. Thing is, I suffered through years of turmoil until Faith forced me to face my demons. If I can help force Erin face hers, no matter how pissed off she might be that I told you, it's worth it."

"Yeah?"

"As long as you have true feelings for her."

"Are you kidding? She's having my baby."

"Changes a lot, doesn't it?"

"Sure. But, the truth? I'd have feelings for her even if she weren't pregnant. She got under my skin like no other woman has in a long time." Nate made a regretful face. "That's between you and me. Erin doesn't exactly know how I feel."

"Exactly?"

"Okay, at all. The way it went down—" He shook off the thought. Nate drilled his new friend with a stare. "How about a deal. Man-to-man. I keep your secrets if you keep mine? For as long as it's necessary."

Brody hung up his cue. "Let's grab a booth."

An hour, the entire tale of the tragedy, and two additional beers each later, Nate sat back and shook his head, squeezing the bridge of his nose between thumb and finger. "I can't believe everything the four of you survived. No wonder your friendship is so strong."

Brody nodded. "A crisis like that, man, it changes everything. Not just your life. Your whole life *perspective*. I can't even explain it." He hiked his chin. "If I didn't have Faith to help me through the rough times, I'd still be floundering. I miss her sister, Mick, every single day. She was my best friend."

"You still feel responsible?"

Brody hiked one shoulder. "I probably always will. But it's lessened some. The guilt. I can get through a day, an hour. I feel like my life has purpose again, like Mick would approve of me and Faith, and that's something."

"What about Erin?"

"I don't know. It's hard to get a read on her, as you well know."

Nate snorted, took a sip of beer.

"She and Kevin were—" he shook his head, then twisted two fingers tightly together "—you know. *That* couple. The ones everyone knew would make it. I can't lie to you, man. Losing him and their baby ripped out a big part of her heart and soul. She's different now."

A combination of sympathy and envy assailed Nate, twisting his gut into a tight knot. He'd never be Kevin, didn't even think he could halfway fill the man's shoes in Erin's eyes. Still, if only he could find a way to help mend her broken parts, he'd move the earth to do so. He wanted her to be happy.

He wanted to be the one to make her happy.

The story made her incomprehensible actions that night and the morning after fall neatly into place. If only he'd known. All the anger he'd felt after the task force meeting, the cutting words he'd used against her at the diner—she hadn't deserved them. If only he could take them all back...

He blew out a breath. "We made a lot of mistakes, Erin and I."

"Everyone makes mistakes. But, this baby— your baby," Brody said, "it's made a huge difference. As rough as the pregnancy's been for Erin emotionally and on her job, it's brought her out of a really dark place. You have to believe that."

Nate swallowed back a lump in his throat. "I don't know what to do next."

"Persist. Be there. Help her even when she tells you to go to hell, which she will. Frequently."

Nate smiled sadly.

"Call her bluffs, 'cause she's an expert at them." He took a big swallow, finishing his beer. "Erin's tough as they come on the outside, which makes her damned good at her career. But inside? She's just like the rest of us, Nate. Vulnerable. Looking for that forever safe place."

"What are the odds she'll let herself find that place with someone other than Kevin?"

Brody aimed the neck of his beer bottle across the table and sucked in one side of his cheek. "That part, my friend, is up to you."

Nate huffed. "In other words, I'm dead in the water."

"Don't be so sure."

"How do you figure?"

"Simple. Erin's always been a hot commodity in these parts." He flipped a hand. "I mean, look at her."

"Yeah." Nate's body reacted almost immediately. No doubts. The physical attraction? Alive and well.

"But, the point is, despite mad interest, she never dated anyone. Not a single guy. Until you." Brody let that sink in.

Nate glanced away. "We didn't exactly *date*."

"Maybe you should, then."

He squinted. "Ask her on a date?"

"Why not?"

As if it would be that easy. Wasn't that like backtracking? *First I'll get you pregnant, then we'll go out for coffee.* There had to be something more. Something that would prove to her how much he respected her. He'd brainstorm the whole problem later. He rolled Brody's idea around in his head. "A date, huh?"

Brody laid his arm along the back of the padded

booth. "I probably don't need to remind you, but she's carrying your kid. So, yes, ask her on a freakin' date. What have you got to lose?"

"Everything. That's the problem."

Brody curled the edges of his mouth down. "Listen, I'm no expert on women, but I do know Erin pretty well. I'd say, if you want to be, you're still afloat. Just keep paddling, brother. Keep paddling."

The next day, Erin felt the overwhelming urge to check on Nate, see how he was settling in. Now that he lived in her airspace, she couldn't stop thinking about him. She had way too much free time on her hands.

She sat in her kitchen, on edge, and listened to one, two, three rings before Nate's voice mail kicked in. She sighed, both disappointed and relieved by the reprieve. She waited through his greeting—where was he? As if she had any business wondering—but after the beep, her heart began to pound. Oh yeah, she had to talk.

Coherently.

Straightening her spine, she cleared her throat. "Um, hi, Nate. It's Erin. Sorry to bother you." *Think, Erin. Think.* "I just, uh, thought we might set up a time to get Boomer and Thug acquainted with my big lug of a dog, and—"

"Hey, you," she heard, after some scrambling. "I couldn't make it to the phone in time."

She smirked, knowing a lie when she heard one. "Right, because your place is so huge. Screening calls, are we?"

He chuckled. "Guilty as charged. I'm working on a new project idea. Figured I could return any business calls after my brainstorm ended."

"Don't let me keep you then."

"No. No. It's business calls I'm avoiding." His voice dropped to a silky tone. "You, I want to talk to."

She smiled, surprisingly pleased by his words.

"Is it okay to ask how you're feeling?" he ventured.

Erin cringed. "Listen, about yesterday. I can't explain it, but sometimes that irritability just demands center stage. I'm not usually prone to such mood swings. It's the whole pregnancy thing."

"No harm, no foul. Truly, you can feel however you want to."

She exhaled, releasing her pent-up worry that he'd decided she was an evil whackjob to be avoided at all costs. "Thank you. He was kicking me all day yesterday, which hurts. It really wears on you."

Silence.

Her throat squeezed.

They still didn't know each other well enough to read silences. "What's wrong?"

"A boy? We're having a boy?"

"Oh, that." She laughed softly. "I don't know. Haven't checked, and I kind of like the idea of being surprised. It's just easier than saying he or she all the time."

"Gotcha."

"I'd tell you, Nate. If I knew."

"I appreciate that." He hesitated. "So, which do you want? Boy or girl?"

"I want whoever this little soul is. I just want a healthy baby. Sounds so cliché." She smiled. "How about you?"

"Same. Although, I won't lie. I've been surrounded by so many females all my life, a boy would be cool."

She nodded. "I can understand that. Especially after what Faith and I put you through yesterday."

"Shoot, woman, that was small potatoes. When I was a clueless teenage boy, all my sisters had their periods at the same time. One week a month, I was the family whipping post, verbal and physical."

She laughed. "I can't believe we're talking about this. How can I ever look them in the eyes?"

"Consider the positive side—I'm not afraid to buy *any* product at the grocery store, if you know what I mean."

"Bonus."

"So, about the beasts—"

Back to business. "Yes. I'd planned to invite you three over now. But, you're busy, and I've already taken up enough of your time."

"Actually, it's not that. I'm going to talk to the condo association about their obsolete 'no animals' rule. I own the place—or will, as soon as we close. As I see it, I should be able to keep my pets as long as they aren't unruly. Every condo owner should."

"Brave move. I wish you the best of luck, but if it doesn't work out, my offer is open-ended."

"Thank you. I'd be lonely without them here, though."

"I know what you mean." She glanced over toward Finn, snoozing tummy-up in a sunbeam.

"If it all works out, what do you think about me hiring Jason to care for them when I travel? The kid obviously liked them, and he's going to need money for college."

Her heart expanded. "Oh, Nate, that's a great idea. Faith will really appreciate you putting your trust in him, and it will do so much for his self-confidence."

"Good. Good. I'll call them later."

They fell into a small silence, and she could hear him shuffling paper on the other end.

"Well, you sound busy. I'll let you get back to work." Strange. She didn't want to hang up.

"Erin, wait. Does Troublesome Gulch have a decent-sized fairgrounds?" he asked.

She blinked, surprised by the out-of-the-ether question, but glad to still be talking to him. "Sure. The county fairgrounds are here. Why?"

"I'll explain later. Can you show the place to me?"

"When?"

"No time like the present. There's a free lunch in it for you if you say yes," he teased.

"Make it free ice cream, and you're on."

"Are you sure? I'm not watchdogging you," he assured, "but you told me you weren't supposed to gain much weight."

"I know." She groaned. "But I've been watching my diet so closely, I feel like one of those skeletal Hollywood starlets, and it's making me cranky. I've held steady at nineteen pounds gained for so long now, I'm starting to feel safe. What are the odds I'll blimp out in the last few weeks?"

"Slim to none, no pun intended. You're far too disciplined for that."

"I'm glad you agree. I'd never do anything to compromise this baby, but I think every pregnant woman deserves at least one serving of ice cream in a nine-month period. Don't you?"

"Absolutely. Ice cream it is." He paused. "Can I pick you up?"

For a split second, she started to suggest separate cars. But they were past that, weren't they? Didn't she want to be? She extended the small olive branch, hoping they'd sail over the hump on their way to true friendship. "Got a pen? I'll give you directions."

The fairgrounds were absolutely perfect. A vast flat area flanked by a half circle of flatiron peaks. He itched to get home and draw up his plan, but despite the short time frame, he wouldn't give up these stolen moments with Erin for the world.

They sat atop a picnic table in a small park they had all to themselves near the center of town, a block or so from the ice-cream parlor. Dappled sunlight shone down on them. A light breeze swirled Erin's dark hair.

She groaned in pleasure at her first bite of ice cream, letting her eyes flutter shut. "Mmm." She swallowed. "I'd kill for this stuff. I really would."

"Should I move a prudent distance away?"

She shook her head, taking another bite through a chuckle. "You indulged my urge, so you're safe."

"Thank goodness." He grinned, sipping from his milk shake. "So, tell me about your family. I've told you all about mine."

"Well, let's see." She thought through another bite. "Mom and Dad have been married forever. They lived here until they both retired two years ago, and now they live in Crested Butte."

"Do you miss them?"

"Of course. But they visit all the time. And I go there. It's not far. They have their dream property, at last. My mom's a potter. She was the art teacher at our high school since I was a kid—the teacher everyone adored. Cagney especially."

"She's an artist?"

"Was. Her dad's kind of a jerk, and strongly opposed an art career, but it's a whole, 'nother long story." She grimaced. "Anyway, Mom finally has her own workshop, with different-sized kilns, all sorts of shelves and drying racks and, most of all, space."

"Cool. Good for her."

Erin nodded. "She's in heaven. Dad was the high school phys ed teacher. Now he works ski patrol part-time. He tried the 'retired old guy' thing, but first of all, he's not that old. Secondly, he drove Mom nuts."

"We men have a knack for that," Nate said, ruefully.

"Yep. I think he grew a little stir-crazy himself." She shrugged. "Anyway, he loves it, and it keeps him in shape and healthy."

"Brothers and sisters?"

"Only child. I always wanted a sister."

He nodded, listening to the birds and studying his and Erin's feet side by side on the picnic bench.

He tried to keep his tone light. "How do they feel about the pregnancy?"

"I knew that part was coming." She eyed him. "They were shocked at first, of course. Since I'm…single. But they couldn't be more excited now. I mean, I'm twenty-nine years old, and they weren't sure I could ever conceive, either, so they'd pretty much given up on the grandparent plan." She shook her head. "This kid is going to be so spoiled, Nate. I have to apologize for them in advance."

"Don't worry, he'll be getting it from both sides. My sisters and Mom?" He rolled his eyes. "Pure insanity."

They shared a smile.

He held her gaze. "Do your parents know about me?"

She paused a beat. "Not…exactly."

He pressed his lips together, nodded. Her words left him beyond disappointed, even though, deep down, he'd been expecting them. His family knew the whole story. Then again, he'd had to explain why he was up and moving to Colorado, seemingly on a whim. They'd rolled with it, as he'd known they would, and were all chomping at the bit to come for a visit and meet Erin. But he begged them to hold off until he got his bearings, figured out what this strange relationship between him and Erin was all about.

"I'm going to tell them," she rushed to add. "It's just, well, they can be old-fashioned. I'm trying to figure out how to explain that we're not a couple and make them realize that it's really okay."

Was it? he wondered, peering over at her. She was so achingly beautiful in the sunshine, humming in ecstasy over her single scoop of ice cream. Simple pleasures. She took his breath away every time he saw her. "Anything I can do to help?"

She quirked her mouth apologetically. "Bear with me? I'm not keeping your identity from them because I'm ashamed of you or anything. If we were together, it would be a whole different story."

If only they were. "No worries. I get the parent thing. But you'll tell them before—"

"Yes. Definitely."

He didn't point out that she'd begun finishing his sentences, but it cheered him. Maybe they did have a chance after all. The challenge was proving he was worth risking her already-broken heart.

She scraped the last vestiges of ice cream from her dish with the pink, plastic spoon and ate it, whimpering when she peered into the empty cup.

"If you weren't here, I'd lick this cup like a shameless dog." She stilled. "Oh."

"What's up?"

"I think the baby liked it as much as I did. Feel."

She reached for his hand without an iota of hesitation, then laid it flat against the side of her belly. Beneath his palm came the press of a tiny foot, once, then again. Harder.

"Ouch," she said, frowning down at her belly with a playful shake of her head. "Little bully."

Unexpectedly, tears of awe rose to his eyes. "He's really a little person in there."

She smiled. Then, noticing how choked up Nate had become, she touched his face. "Amazing, isn't it? And kind of freaky, if you want the whole truth. Hard to explain, but I sort of feel like one of those Russian nesting dolls, where you pop one open, and a smaller version's inside."

He could only hope their baby was a smaller version of Erin. Talk about a gorgeous kid. He clenched his jaws, fighting back the flashes of emotion bursting inside him. "Thank you. For sharing that."

"You don't have to thank me. He's your baby, too."

Their gazes locked.

He had so much he wanted to say to her, but he didn't know how to start, or if his words would even be welcomed. He opened his mouth. Nothing emerged.

"Shh." She laid a finger along his lips. "You don't have to say anything."

"God, Erin," he said, his tone husky. "The truth

is, I would freeze this moment if I could, and I'm not ashamed to admit it."

He impulsively pulled her into his arms, burying his face into the soft heat of her neck. She stiffened initially, then let herself relax against him, smoothing her hands up and down his back. He felt the pulse in her neck against his lips and kissed it.

She allowed it. Even seemed to nuzzle closer.

"Ah, Nate." She sighed.

"I know."

This was one moment he didn't mind being in.

Chapter Ten

She'd never imagined a simple scoop of ice cream could become an emotional bridge between two people. But, following their afternoon in the park, her connection with Nate shifted in a million subtle ways. They began talking on the phone, then hanging out together, as though doing so went without saying. Little by little, the omnipresent awkwardness between them dissipated.

They watched her favorite reality TV show side by side on his couch or hers in the evenings, after which she'd read and he'd work. He and Boomer joined her and Finn on her daily morning walks. And, their conversation grew easier every day.

More importantly, their silences transformed from clumsy to comfortable and compatible— something she hadn't expected to happen so soon, if at all. She didn't know what it all meant, exactly, just that it felt good.

The first time she read a whole chapter of a book without commenting, and without feeling self-conscious about lying there in silence on his couch while he worked, she knew they'd reached a different level. But, a different level of *what?* That was the question. All for the baby? Platonic? Platonic with options? Romantic? Try as she might, she couldn't get a read.

There'd been no further physical intimacy. Not even another kiss on the neck, although she relived that delicious first one as she closed her eyes to sleep each night. And yet, despite their obvious physical distance, she still felt closer to him than ever.

She'd even gone with him to shop for nursery furniture for his condo. Of course, that trip ended abruptly when she'd succumbed to an emotional meltdown at the thought of being away from the baby overnight.

The pregnancy hormones hit, and BOOM— from normal to sobbing and shaking in a matter of seconds, just as they were about to choose between the natural wood or sweet little painted crib. But, reminiscent of the bar scene that fateful night, Nate had whisked her out of the furniture store immediately, comforted her until she'd recovered her composure, and they hadn't brought up shared custody issues since.

Time for that later, she supposed.

All these snippets combined added up to no more than a dip of her toe into the water of their new, strange compromise, but so far she hadn't felt the urge to pull back.

For her, that was huge.

As amazing as it seemed, in a couple short weeks, Nate had begun to feel like a fixture in her life. Dinner without him now struck her as odd. They didn't plan it, they just did it. Her house, his house, a restaurant. Didn't matter. Finn refused to walk now until his new beloved buddy, Boomer, showed up.

Life felt somehow fuller with Nate around.

Still, there was so much they didn't know about each other, which amounted to a huge concrete wall between them, at least in her mind. And she had no idea how to breach it.

Her friends, wisely, stayed out of their blossoming whatever-it-was...*relationship,* she supposed, was as good a word as any. Even matchmaker Faith had, surprisingly, kept her trap shut, which was surely due to Brody's thumbscrew influence. Erin appreciated the space.

But when Cagney invited the whole crew to her loft for her monthly, much anticipated dinner party, Erin and Nate sent a positive RSVP—as a couple. Or a duo. Or, like, they were going to show up in the same car together. Whatever.

The point is, it didn't feel weird.

Which, in and of itself, was weird.

Nevertheless, when the evening of the dinner party arrived, nerves bounced around inside Erin's tummy like a bevy of racquetballs with minds of their own. It was the first time all her friends, as a group, would observe her and Nate in this new "format," and she hoped that didn't spell disaster with a capital *D*. Things were still fragile between the two of them, despite the progress they'd made. She needed time to work it all out in her own mind before she spoke about it aloud with anyone. Really, what would she say?

She'd borrowed the least maternity-looking sundress in the pack from her coworker, Ginny Luther's, excellent pregnancy closet, appreciating the way the V-neck halter highlighted her enhanced cleavage. The deep turquoise perfectly matched Nate's eyes, which she hadn't planned. It also matched the beaded sandals and drawstring handbag, which she had.

Hair done, makeup on, she twirled a bit in front of the mirror, surprised that she felt sexy and filled with anticipation. She hadn't felt sexy in…well, forever about covered it. And she hadn't anticipated a date—if you could call this a date—since high school.

Probably because she hadn't had one since.

Pathetic.

She was leaning toward the mirror slipping simple hoop earrings in when the doorbell rang.

Her heart revved.

Finn barked, launched himself from the window seat in her bedroom, and clickity-clacked toward the entryway.

"It's unlocked," she called out, knowing Nate would hear her through the open windows.

She heard the ancient door hinges creak, then the murmured sounds of Nate talking to Finn as she gave herself a final once-over.

Oh, God. It felt like a date.

Self-consciousness hit her like a rogue wave, knocking her flat, but hell, it would have to do.

She took in a deep, cleansing breath.

She could do this.

She *wanted* to do this.

Grabbing her handbag off the end of the bed before she lost her nerve, she snicked off the ceiling fan and headed out. She found Nate by the front door, bent forward giving Finn an excellent scratch behind the ears. Finn looked love-struck, the big sap.

She couldn't help but smile. "Hey."

Nate glanced up and froze. His eyes widened. "Whoa." He straightened slowly, taking in her appearance with an appreciative gleam in his eyes.

Thrilled by his response but determined to keep it casual, she said, "I take that to mean I don't look like a big, turquoise balloon float from the Macy's Parade?"

"Far from it. You look amazing."

"Amazing's probably a stretch, but you're a generous man. Thank you." She reached into the jar of dog treats on the hallway console table and pulled out a biscuit, handing it to Finn, patting him on the head.

As the dog crunched away, she assessed Nate. "You look pretty darn amazing yourself," she said, in as light a tone as she could manage considering how dizzy she'd become in his presence.

Amazing? Understatement.

He wore khaki pants and a loose, black, short-sleeved shirt that made his eye color stand out even more than usual. Casual, masculine, yum-yum-yummy. His hair had been trimmed, but his face bore an attractive amount of groomed stubble that begged to be touched. He looked like a movie star—no lie.

And he was her *date*.

Impulsively, she leaned forward and kissed him on the cheek, inhaling the citrus scent of his skin as she did so. Just a friendly greeting, she told herself. As she pulled away, he grabbed her elbow to stop her. Their gazes met, held. His darkened, then dropped to her lightly glossed lips. Pure primal craving bound them together.

Her throat cinched, and all the key parts of her body reacted.

Moving closer, he kissed her gently. Once, then again, letting his mouth linger against hers. "Thank you."

She swallowed, the sensual stimulation of his stubble and warm breath against her mouth leaving her nerves humming. "You're welcome. Ready?"

"You bet I am," he said, cryptically, leaving her to wonder exactly what question he'd been answering.

Once they were seat belted in and on the road, the tsunami of heightened sexual awareness between them retreated, thank goodness, but the emotional destruction remained in her brain. She needed to regroup. She didn't want to walk into the party surrounded by a cloud of pheromones, after all. Her friends would be watching them closely enough as it was.

Focus on the present.

"Do you know the way?" Well, it sounded

casual enough. Yay, her. She surreptitiously admired his hand, draped over the top of the steering wheel. She knew what those skilled hands felt like on her body, inside her—

Stop it, Erin.

He tipped his head to the side, seemingly unaware of her turmoil. "I looked it up on computer mapping, but it appeared to be a warehouse." He shrugged. "I probably had the address wrong."

Erin smiled. "Nope, that's the place."

He flashed her a quizzical glance. "Cagney lives in a warehouse?"

"A warehouse *loft*," she corrected. "Her single act of rebellion against her father in the past twelve years, which rocks. She doesn't rebel much anymore, unfortunately, but back in the day, she was the queen of it. Man, was her dad pissed when she bought that old building," she added, savoring the memory.

"I can appreciate rebellion, but why would she want to live in a warehouse in the first place?"

"Wait until you see it," Erin said. "She's the renovation queen. The ground level is still unfinished, but she lives on the second and third floors. It's probably the most amazing residence in the entire Gulch. Plus, Cagney always wanted to live in a huge loft. Of course," she added ruefully, "that was when she still planned on being a working artist and using half the loft as her studio."

Nate flicked on his blinker, then merged onto the Gulch's main drag. "What happened with that?"

"Long story. But the bottom line is, her dad fought so hard against it that she eventually lost her will."

"Her dad sounds like a piece of work."

"Totally. And he's the chief of police."

He flashed her another quick glance before refocusing on the road. "She works for the guy?"

"Yep." Erin shook her head. "It's a damn shame, too. Cagney's a great cop. Must be in her blood. But I don't think she's happy. My mom still waxes poetic about little Casey's unbelievable talent and what a crime it is to waste it. But, she had utterly no support from home."

Nate sucked one side of his cheek in, sympathetic but still exuding optimism. "Well, she's got her own home now, and it's never too late. She's only twenty-nine. Maybe she'll go back to it."

Erin hadn't mentioned the heartbreak. The betrayal. The loss that led up to Cagney's total abandonment of her life's passion. So much loss in Erin's little circle of friends. Her heart squeezed for Cagney. For all of them, and she sighed. "I don't know, Nate. Sometimes, for some things, it is too late."

Before he could comment further, she pointed up toward the huge building they approached. "There it is. We can just park anywhere."

Festive lights shone through the floor-to-ceiling windows, and Erin found herself excited about another celebratory night of good food and laughter with her friends. And with Nate.

In fact, she realized as they parked and got out, it wouldn't feel complete without him.

Just as she'd suspected, everything had changed.

Dinner had been spectacular, not to mention low in both fat and carbs in deference to Erin's weight gain directive. Not that you could tell from the incredible flavors. She loved Cagney's quiet consideration of her.

Erin and Nate hadn't been able to avoid slipping into their newfound comfort with each other. She even caught herself finishing a few of his sentences, and vice versa. She found each of them watching the other as he or she spoke to the group. The way couples do. And throughout the evening, she sensed her friends, one by one, noticing, sizing things up.

After Nate's copious compliments on the loft while they enjoyed coffee and dessert, Cagney had offered to give him the full tour and regale him with the tale of her solo, two-year-long renovations. Erin knew Cagney loved to talk about all she'd done—it was as artsy as she'd allowed herself to be since prom night. Though he'd seen it all before, Brody tagged along. He and Nate had really hit it off. Maybe because they were the only two guys in the mix.

Meanwhile, she, Lexy and Faith cleared the table, chattering about this and that as they did so. Shoes, TV, work gossip—all the normal stuff.

Erin set the last large stack of stoneware next to the sink and turned around, coming face-to-face with a determined-looking Faith and a highly intrigued Lexy. She lifted her brows. "What's up, Pip? Lex?" As if she didn't know.

"Yeah, I think that's our line," Faith said, crossing her arms over her distended belly.

"I don't know what you're talking about."

"Sure you don't, doll face." Lexy grinned. "Seems like you and Mr. Hottie are getting along better."

"Well, that's not exactly true. We've always gotten along fine. I mean, except for when he popped into town unexpectedly and found this." She framed her belly with her hands. "But you can't blame him for that."

"You know what we mean," Faith said.

Erin toyed with the idea of blowing off their probing questions, but after a wonderful evening ensconced in the circle of her pals, she suddenly craved the sounding board of her best girlfriends. God knew, she wasn't figuring this thing out so well on her own.

She leaned back against the counter. "Yeah,

well." She sighed, crossing her arms as best she could with this gigantic belly to contend with. "We've been spending a lot of time together lately. For the baby's sake," she added.

"What about for Mommy's sake?" Faith pushed.

"It's not that easy." Erin bit the corner of her lip, glancing around to make sure Cagney and the guys were nowhere near. "He doesn't know anything about the burns. Kevin. My other baby." She sighed. "Kind of limits true intimacy when I can't even talk about my biggest life events, you know?"

"So, talk about them. What's the issue?"

Lexy glanced at Faith, a chastising look on her face. "Faith, come on. We all have to do scary things in our own time. Your own husband should've taught you that."

Faith blew out a breath. "I know. He did, and I do understand your hesitation, no matter how impatient I seem." She beseeched Erin. "But, if you could see how that man looks at you, Erin, how the two of you together look to the rest of us." She hugged herself. "Nate is exactly what you need to help you heal. You may not see it, but he's been so good for you already."

"I do see it," Erin admitted. "But there's Kevin…" Her words choked off, and she reached a hand up to cover her mouth.

Lexy reached out and held Erin's other hand. Faith stepped forward and cupped the sides of

Erin's face. "Sweetie, we all know Kevin was The One, and you two had an amazing ride, while it lasted." A pause. "But…he's gone. He's been gone for a long, long time. He's in Heaven with Mick and Randy and…whatever that guy's name was, Cagney's date." She cringed. "God, that's awful. He's irrevocably part of us, and yet I have this mental block about him that's so unfair. We should know the poor kid's name."

"Tad. Tad Rivers," Lexy said.

"Tad, right." Faith refocused on Erin. "Kevin's with them now. Not with us."

Tears rose to Erin's eyes. "I still love him, though. Just because he's…" She couldn't say it. "That love hasn't gone away."

"You always will love him, and you should. No one thinks you should stop loving Kevin."

"That would be like asking me to stop loving Mick," Faith said.

"But it *is* possible to love again," Lexy said softly. "A real here-and-now love, with the relationship, the family, the dogs, the whole nine. Shoot, you and Nate are ninety percent there. You even have a bunny."

Erin sniffed, glancing down at Lexy. "Yeah? And when are you going to take your own advice, chickie?"

Lexy lifted her chin. "Someday," she said,

breezily. "But, we're talking about you, so stop trying to change the subject. You're the one giving birth in a few weeks."

Erin thought for a moment, then shuddered. "I can't imagine how to even begin that conversation with Nate. It's all just too painful and unmanageable." Erin pointed toward the sitting area anchored in the center of the wide-open space with a deep red area rug. "Can we please sit? My legs are aching."

The two women ushered her to the love seat, where Erin moved the coffee table back so Lexy could maneuver her chair closer. She pulled up directly in front of Erin, then patted her lap. "Put your feet up here. I may no longer be the dancing queen, but I give a killer foot rub."

"Me next?" Faith asked, wistfully.

"Of course."

No arguments from Erin. She slipped out of the beaded sandals and lifted her feet to rest on Lexy's lap, groaning in pleasure when the magic fingers took over.

"So," Lexy said, once they were settled. "How about I ask some simple yes or no questions?"

Erin acquiesced with a nod.

"Do you have feelings for him?"

She sucked in a breath, held it, then blew it out. "Yes."

"Does he have feelings for you?"

"That, I don't know." She pulled her mouth to the side. "We've been spending a lot of time together, sure, but we don't discuss relationship stuff. At all. And we don't—" She rolled her hand.

"Oh, he has feelings for you," Faith said, sounding one hundred percent sure.

Erin cut her a sharp glance, her chest squeezing. "How do you know? Did Brody say something?" They *had* been hanging out quite a bit.

"He hasn't said a word. You know how guys are."

Disappointment drained through Erin.

"I can just tell," Faith continued.

"You're such a matchmaker," Lexy teased.

"Lex, they're having a baby together. I want her to be madly in love, like I am. It's the way it should be."

Lexy held up a hand. "Oh, I'm not disagreeing. Anyone can see he's into you, Erin."

"So? What should I do? And don't say throw my body at him." She splayed her hands on her distended middle. "At this point, that is *not* an option."

"How about taking an even bigger risk?" Lexy asked.

"Bigger than getting naked when I look like a beached whale? A burned beached whale at that?" She arched her brows. "This ought to be rich."

"Open up to him about your past." Lexy paused,

searching her face. "Take the chance and tell him about Kev, the baby, your scars."

"God." Erin covered her face with both hands, feeling sick to her stomach. "I'm so scared. What if—?"

"What if what?" Faith spread her arms wide, leaning closer for emphasis. "Isn't it better to know before you fall even further in love with him?"

"I never said I was in love with him," Erin muttered, as her whole body heated.

Her friends gave her indulgent smiles.

"No matter what happens, you'll always have your friends," Faith said. "So you'll be no worse off if he freaks out and leaves town."

Surprisingly, Erin found this to be cold comfort. How wrong Faith was. She couldn't imagine losing Nate now, no matter how little of him she had at this point, no matter how superficial. No. It was easier to keep her secrets, live in comfortable denial, and keep him close by for as long as it lasted. The risk? Too scary. She couldn't talk to Nate about her past. Not yet. She'd come up with another way to bring them closer…somehow.

She smiled tightly, easing her feet to the floor while hoping to put this conversation to rest, at least for now. "I'll try. You guys are the best. Thank you."

"We love you. We want to know what's up," Lexy said.

Guilt stabbed Erin. "I know I've been...distant. I'm just trying to figure things out. But I'll keep you in the loop from here on out. Promise." She pointed toward Lexy's lap. "Your turn, Faith. Be prepared for the foot massage of a lifetime."

Erin had been uncharacteristically pensive the whole ride home. He didn't know why. He decided to try for some easy conversation, lighten things up.

"You were right. Cagney's loft is amazing."

She stirred, as though out of deep thoughts. "Isn't it? As much as I adore my cute, 1900s farmhouse, I envy her that place. It's so hip. Such a showplace."

Her words and the enthusiasm behind them didn't match up. He reached over and laid his palm lightly on her thigh. "I had a great evening. Thanks for taking me."

"You're always welcome."

"Did you? Have a good time?"

"Yes. Great," she said, way too monotone for the Erin he'd come to know.

A pause. "Everything okay, honey?"

She leaned her head back. "I'm just tired. Long night."

He nodded. Another lag in the conversation. "I really love your friends."

She rolled her head to the side and flashed him a sad smile. "The feeling is mutual. Believe me."

That warmed his heart. But he wished Erin loved him even half as much as her friends did. He patted her thigh and put his hand back on the steering wheel. "Let me get you home so you can relax, put your feet up. Get some rest."

"Nate?"

"Mmm?"

"Have you ever been in love?" Her voice wavered on the question.

He tipped his head side to side, eyes firmly on the road. "More like infatuation. Not that I'm knocking infatuation, mind you. But I've never asked anyone to marry me. Never been consumed with wanting to be with one woman above all others." *Until now*.

She nodded. He couldn't read the gesture. Part of him wanted to lob the question back at her, but he already knew the answer, and he didn't see the point in pushing. She'd tell him when she told him. Period.

"I've been busy building my career," he explained. "You know how that goes."

"Sure. I understand."

"Here we are," he said, pulling into her driveway. The gravel crunched beneath his tires. "Home sweet home."

He cut the engine, and for a long stretch, they just sat there. Finally, he cleared his throat. "Let me walk you in."

"Okay."

They got out of the car and headed toward the house in silence. Erin fumbled with the key, her hands shaky.

He laid his hand on hers. "Let me."

She handed the key over without argument and stepped back. He opened the door, then stood aside so she could enter before him. Finn rose from his dog bed for the requisite ear scratches and love, before returning to his favorite spot. Three spins in a circle, and he was out cold again, with a big doggy sigh.

He set her key ring on the console and dipped his chin, studying her. "Sure you're okay? I don't mean to keep nagging you, but it seems like you aren't feeling well. Or maybe like something's weighing on your mind."

"I feel fine, really. For a huge preggo, that is."

"Well, okay." He paused, hoping for more. "I guess I should go then."

"Wait." She flicked her tongue over her lips nervously. "Do you remember that night? At the hotel?"

"All too well."

"Not that part. I mean, when I asked you to hold me?"

He nodded.

Looking as though she were garnering her courage, she stepped forward and wrapped her arms around him, resting her face against his chest. "I need that again," she whispered.

He gladly embraced her. "What's going on?"

"I'm not sure. I just don't want you to leave."

"Aw, Erin—"

"Please?" She tipped her face up and rained small kisses on his lips. "I don't want to be here alone, no offense to Finn."

He didn't want to leave, either. Ever. Still, he had to be sure she was saying what he hoped she was saying. "I could call Cagney for you. Or Lexy."

"No." She paused, her rapid pulse visible in the side of her neck. "What I meant was, I don't want to be here alone without you. If you need to go get Boomer and Thug and bring them—"

"They're fine."

"Then—?"

"What are we doing?" he whispered, smoothing the backs of his fingers down her silky soft cheek.

"I don't know. I don't know yet. I just want you to hold me. I want to fall asleep in your arms. If that's okay with you."

"Sweet girl, it's more than okay."

He swore he could feel the tension drain out of her. "Good. Thank you."

"When are you going to stop thanking me?"

"When I stop feeling indebted. And guilty."

He threaded his fingers into the sides of her

hair, then leaned in and kissed her. Gently at first, deeper when he felt her response, the vibrations of her moan against his face. After several long minutes of sensual exploration, he pulled back. "You're driving the bus on this crazy trip, Erin. If you need me, say the word."

"Okay, I need you," she said, in a bereft whisper. "But, God, if you only knew. I don't deserve you."

"That," he said, guiding her toward her bedroom, "is where we'll have to agree to disagree. Now, let's get you ready for bed. You need your rest."

She stiffened. "Wait. I can do it."

"Erin," he said lightly, "I wasn't suggesting that I tear your clothes off. I'm well aware that's not what this is about."

She exhaled. "Okay. Sorry. I'm just a little on edge." She paused at the bedroom door, clasping the jamb with one hand. "I'll be a minute."

"Take your time." He held her chin with two gentle fingers, leaning in to nip at her luscious lips. "I'm not going anywhere."

"Swear?" she whispered.

"I am absolutely here for you. And that's a promise."

Chapter Eleven

She and Nate fell into the habit of spending their nights together at her house or his. They held each other as they drifted off, kissed some. Nothing more than that and, unfortunately, no in-depth conversations.

Her wall, it seemed, remained.

She was no closer to knocking it down.

A week prior to the dreaded Fourth of July fireworks show—something she and Nate never discussed—Chief Dresden called to inform Erin about an emergency meeting of the task force that had been called for that day. She had two hours to get ready. Granted, she and Nate avoided the whole fireworks issue by tacit agreement, but it still seemed odd he hadn't mentioned it before he'd left that morning. She supposed it could've been a surprise to him, too. In any case, her curiosity was piqued.

She showered quickly, dressed in her borrowed Class-A maternity uniform, then headed to the city building. After entering the conference room, she slid into the seat next to Brody, jostling her shoulder against his as a hello.

He smiled at her. "Hey, you."

"What's with the emergency task force meeting?" she whispered.

"Your guess is as good as mine. I just got word a couple hours ago."

"Same here."

He lifted his chin toward the man who stood at the front of the room, readying his equipment as they awaited the arrival of everyone else. "Nate didn't mention anything?"

"Nope." She shook her head in feigned annoyance, then leaned in to rasp, "I'm having a kid with the guy, and I don't even get insider info. How jacked up is that?"

"Having a *baby* with him doesn't merit insider info." He held up a finger. "Now, having hot, sweaty *jungle sex* with him? Whole different story."

"Do not make me kill you."

"Kidding! Only kidding." Brody smirked. "I don't know why we're here. Maybe the city manager got a brain and realized risking a wildfire was the quickest, surest way to lose his seat during the next election."

Erin huffed. "Yeah, sure. And maybe I'm pregnant with a litter of puppies."

"Cool, can I have the runt? Hope would dig a playmate," he said, referring to the puppy he'd bought for Faith when he proposed.

She pierced him with a withering stare. "How does your wife even tolerate you, Austin?"

He waggled his eyebrows. "Mad skills. What more can I say?"

"Nothing." She held up a hand and pretended disgust. "News flash—you shouldn't mention sex to a ready-to-pop pregnant woman, and you've done it twice now in a matter of two minutes. For that matter, you should *never* mention it to your wife's best friend."

"You started it. Besides, how do you know I was referring to sex, Assumption Queen?"

"Duh. You're a guy, aren't you?"

"Good point." He grinned shamelessly.

Their banter ceased as the mayor and city manager walked in, greeted Nate, nodded to the rest of them and took their seats. They looked as expectant as everyone else on the committee.

Now her curiosity really kicked up a notch. If *they* hadn't called the meeting…

"Thanks for taking time out of your busy days, everyone," Nate began. "You're probably wondering what this is all about, so let's get to it." He glanced at the secretary. "Polly?"

Nate had known about the meeting, Erin marveled. And he hadn't said word one. She didn't know how to feel about that.

Polly doused the lights. The projection screen eased its way down from the ceiling. As it descended, Nate continued.

"At my request, my researchers conducted an in-depth analysis of the fire danger this year, and we've concluded that a live fireworks show would pose too great a risk to the dry forest, not to mention the town proper." He paused. "Folks, bottom line is, it's simply not worth it."

Hushed exclamations of surprise rose from the darkness. Stunned but thrilled, Erin glanced around at the shadows of the other people in the room.

A silvery light hit the screen, casting Nate in a magical glow. "Before all the questions I'm sure you have, I'd like to assure you that Walker Pyrotechnics has no intentions of abandoning Troublesome Gulch. As most of you know, I live here now." He smiled. "I have a vested interest in the community."

"Yeah, but what are we supposed to do?" Walt Hennessy asked, blustery as usual. "July Fourth is a week away. There's no time to hire another pyrotechnics company this late in the game."

"That's what I'm here to show you. Another option. All I ask is that you keep open minds." Nate pointed a remote at his laptop. "In addition to traditional pyrotechnic events, Walker provides numerous alternative technologies, two of which could far surpass the excitement of a standard fireworks display. Not to mention, they'll be a lot safer."

The screen came to life, showing a mountain as the background for a spectacular light show.

A collective gasp rose from the group.

Erin recognized that range. It surrounded the fairgrounds. She couldn't believe it. The project he'd been working on so diligently had been for them. A rush of emotion swirled in her chest as she looked from the screen to Nate. Happiness, gratitude, other feelings she didn't dare name. He might not understand her vehement disapproval of the fireworks show, but he cared. Enough to find a way around them this year, and that touched her in ways she couldn't even voice.

A lump rose in her throat.

"This technology is called VisionPlex, a high-resolution projection system capable of shooting images onto 3-D surfaces, such as the mountains cupping the county fairgrounds."

"How does it work?" asked Commander Bresil, the representative from the police department.

"It's a process that involves simultaneous imaging from numerous high-tech projectors working in conjunction with one another. The options for the images are as endless as our imaginations. You want safe fireworks? You've got them. This technology has been used on the Academy Awards and Emmy shows, among others."

"Wow," said Commander Bresil, clearly impressed.

"We tested it on the fairgrounds last week, as you can see. We used images of traditional fireworks bursts, but that's just one option." He paused, letting the screen speak for itself. "Let me assure you, it's even more sensational live. To enhance it, we'd also use FogScreen technology along the sides, to frame out the show."

"Which is?" Brody asked.

"FogScreen is a device that produces a wall onto which more images can be projected. A wall," he added with a smile, "of misted water. Much safer in light of this fire season, I'm sure you'll agree. FogScreen technology is the innovation of the decade in the special effects world."

"What's the catch?" Walt Hennessey asked.

"No catch. But here's the best part." Nate rocked slightly on his feet, a smug smile on his face. "We'd be the first city in the nation to use these technologies in an outdoor alternative Fourth of July event. Little old Troublesome Gulch— imagine that? Environmentally conscious. Cutting edge, not to mention spectacular. The total package, if I do say so myself."

"We stand to make history," said Mayor Ron Blackman, with wonder in his voice.

"Bingo," said Nate, pointing toward him.

Erin could do nothing more than sit back and watch. Her heart felt full to bursting for the thought Nate had put into this idea. He spoke so passionately, captivating the whole room. Well, except for, perhaps, Hennessey, but that was to be expected.

Watching Nate, so sexy in his element, she sighed.

Brody jostled her with his shoulder and whispered, "Stop looking like a lovesick sophomore."

"Oh, shut up." She scrunched her nose at him.

"What about the sound? The flash-bang? The oohs and aahs?" Hennessey asked, his tone almost plaintive.

Erin accidentally scoffed, but covered it just as fast with a fake cough into her hand. The city manager had always been known as a whiny control freak. Even he couldn't deny this was the best choice for Troublesome Gulch, but he'd darn well try.

Now, if it had been his idea in the *first* place…

Ah, gotta love politics.

"Sound's included," Nate assured the man. "Music, laser, special effects—all tailored to what we, as a committee, decide. Polly?"

The secretary flipped the lights back on.

Nate spread his arms. "As always, it's your choice. I know we'd have to work quickly, but I have a lot of jumping-off points. Walker Pyrotechnics simply can't stand behind a fireworks show with the liability so high, though. My two cents?"

He paused.

The entire group held their breath.

"Why risk everything during one of the worst fire danger seasons we've seen in years when you have the opportunity to put Troublesome Gulch in the news with something this unique?"

"What about cost differences?" Brody asked, playing devil's advocate. Erin knew he was one hundred percent behind the light show.

"Technically, the VisionPlex and FogScreen alternative would almost triple the cost, but I don't plan to charge the city an extra cent. Consider it my gift to my new hometown. A hometown I do not want to see go up in flames."

More murmured excitement.

"Not only that, but the Pinecone and a couple of other local restaurants I contacted have agreed to provide boxed picnic meals, gratis. A community-wide effort for safety. What more can you ask for?"

He crossed his arms over his chest and looked to each one of them, his eyes gleaming when they met Erin's. "So. Do we mitigate the fire danger and give the city something really special this year?"

"I vote, yes," said Mayor Blackman quickly, shrugging when Walt threw him an incredulous glare.

"Absolutely," said Brody, the same time as Erin. They laughed.

"Copycat," she whispered.

One after another, everyone eagerly agreed to the alternative show, until the whole room sat staring at Walt Hennessey, who couldn't hold back his pout. "Well, if you all think it's a decent alternative…"

"Not decent. It's a fantastic alternative. Ground-breaking," Erin emphasized. She could see the others nodding in her peripheral vision but kept her focus on the recalcitrant city manager. "Let's give the Gulch a legacy beyond the infamous prom night tragedy, Walt, which is just about all we're known for anymore. It's about time, don't you think?"

Hennessey seemed to roll this around in his head, most likely calculating how the change would reflect on his position personally. Finally, he threw up his hands. "Okay, Walker. Looks like I'm outvoted. You're on." He released a peevish sigh. "I'll arrange a press conference to let the citizens know."

"Excellent. If you'd like, I can have my people write up some media releases, Walt, since we're intimately acquainted with the technology."

"Fine." Walt pouted. "I'd like to read everything before it goes out, though."

"Of course," Nate said. "I wouldn't think of handling it any other way." He smiled at the group. "I'm glad we could settle this so quickly, and I applaud your progressiveness. We'll need to meet tomorrow to iron out some of the details. But, I promise, you won't regret this."

The task force members dwindled away one by one until only Brody, Erin and Nate remained. Nate was at the front of the large room. Erin fussed around and took her time at the other end, although she only had to pick up her purse and her information folder and leave. It had to be pretty obvious she was stalling.

"Want me to walk you out, Er?" Brody the Clueless said.

She shot a glance toward Nate and lowered her tone to be sure Nate couldn't hear them. "If you don't mind, I want to have a word with Nate first."

Brody half sat on the edge of the table, casually crossing his feet. "Okay, I can wait."

"No," she said, a bit too quickly. She felt the heat rush into her complexion. "I mean, you don't have to."

His face spread into a slow leer, and he waggled his brows. "Well, hot damn, DeLuca," Brody said under his breath. "Want me to lock the conference room doors behind me?"

She lifted her chin. "Oh, be quiet. I said *talk*."

"I know what you *said*." Brody leaned in. "Just in case you wondered, I approve completely."

"Gosh, I can rest easy now," she said, in a droll tone. "Thanks."

"Seriously, give him a chance, Erin," Brody said, as he pushed away from the table. "I remember you telling me you wanted to take the scary steps, to find your way out of the darkness, like I did."

She angled her gaze away, crossed her arms tightly and rested them on her baby bulge. "Yeah? So?"

"It's not easy, sweetheart." He chucked her under the chin gently. "Believe me, I know. But it's worth it. And Nate's a damn good guy. I befriended him initially because you asked us to. But, after getting to know him, he and I would've been friends anyway."

She bestowed a sincere smile. "I'm glad."

He spread his arms. "Look what he pulled off today. No more fire danger worry. He's top-notch."

"I know. I'm just not sure I'm ready for more steps. He might not even be interested." The thought made her feel ill.

"How will you ever know if you don't try?" Brody cocked one eyebrow to punctuate his rhetorical question, then squeezed her shoulder and headed out.

The door closed behind him, and Nate looked up from where he'd been packing up his equipment. "Still here?"

She hesitated at the back of the room. "Is that okay?"

He grinned. "Of course."

How will you know if you don't try?

Brody's question rang in her ears, thumped in her heart. The damn man had a point. Shoring up her resolve, Erin strode toward Nate as confidently as a lumbering Winnebago in an ugly uniform could. She stopped directly in front of him. He looked up, questions in his gorgeous turquoise eyes.

"Can I help you?" he asked, playfully.

"You already did." With that, she took his face in both of her hands and kissed him. Deeply.

Wow.

She couldn't be less interested in sex at this

point in her pregnancy, but damn if that kiss didn't set a deep, primal throb in motion in spite of her. When she pulled away, his eyes were dark with desire, too.

"What was that for?"

"To thank you."

"You're welcome." He set his remote pointer aside and pulled her against him. "Thank me anytime. For anything."

"Nate, honestly. I've been having nightmares about that damned fireworks display, but no one in city management was going to listen to me." She expelled a breath, searching for words. "What you did, coming up with an alternative, and an amazing one at that—" she shook her head in wonder "—you have no idea what that means to me."

For a few moments, he seemed to battle with his next comment. "Actually, I do."

Confusion drew her forehead into a small frown. "What do you mean?"

"I did the whole thing for you. Because of you." He grasped her upper arms and leaned back, studying her. "Before I explain, how are the hormones raging today?"

She shrugged out of his grasp and whomped him on the chest, laughing as she did so. "Shut up and tell me."

"Okay. It's about time anyway." His shoulders

raised with a deep breath, then dropped. "I know everything, Erin. About your prom night, what happened."

Her eyes widened. A million different feelings tumbled through her in a split second, leaving her breathless. "How?" she managed to choke out.

"It accidentally slipped out in conversation."

"Brody," she said, shaking her head.

He pressed his lips together. "Please don't blame him. He would never violate your confidence. He just assumed I knew since we'd... been intimate."

"Oh. Of course." She stared at the floor. "How long have you known?"

"Awhile." He paused, lowered his tone. "I wish you'd told me."

She pushed out a frustrated sound. "How do you tell someone that? How?"

He pulled her against him, wrapping her in a hug, smoothing his palms down her back. "I understand your fear. But, had I known—" a sigh "—some of the things I said in anger when I first found out about the baby—"

"It's okay." She rested her cheek against his chest, melting into the embrace, inhaling his now-familiar scent. "I deserved them."

"No, you didn't. I'm sorry."

"I'm sorry I haven't said anything. I've never

been in this position before, and I honestly didn't know how."

"It's okay."

"That night…I don't know what I would've done if you'd been, I don't know, disgusted."

"Ah, Erin." He kissed the top of her head, reached up to stroke her hair. "I wish you could get inside my head so you could see yourself through my eyes. You grabbed my attention the moment you walked into the bar that night. Everyone else melted away. If you had any clue how beautiful you are."

"I'm not, though. You haven't seen—"

"I don't care." He pulled back and hunkered down slightly, holding her upper arms in his hands and forcing her to look at him directly. "Not one bit. You make my breath catch every time you walk in a room, do you know that?"

"Man, you're easy."

"No. Don't try to joke your way out of this. You're…you're special, scars or no scars." He shrugged. "Hell, do you think I'm physically perfect?"

"Uh, yes," she said, with sarcasm in her tone.

"You do?" he said, sounding both pleasantly surprised and distracted by her answer. "Sweet."

She shouldered away from him, but he pulled her back into an embrace, laughing. He held her there in his arms, rocking slowly. The tone sobered. "Listen to me. This is hard, but it all has to be said sometime, so…here goes. I know I'm not…Kevin."

"Oh, God." She sucked a breath, buried her face against his chest.

"It's okay," he rushed to say. "It really is. I'm not trying to replace him."

"You don't have to say this," she pleaded.

"Yes. I do."

Ashamed, she held on tightly, wadding the back of his shirt in her hands.

"I can accept not being the love of your life, Erin. I'm secure enough in who I am for that, okay?"

"But—"

He laid a hand on the back of her head. "Please let me finish."

She felt ill, but didn't continue to protest.

"We're having a baby. And we've become friends easily. Closer than friends. Even you have to admit that."

"Yes," she whispered.

"I just want a chance. I know I said I didn't care if you and I had any kind of relationship that day at the Pinecone. I didn't mean it. That was *my* lie." He paused. "You crushed me when you left that hotel room."

She looked up at him, chin quivering. "God, Nate—"

"Shh. I'm not asking for another apology, and I'm not going to bring up that damned note for the rest of our lives, okay?"

She nodded.

"I just want you to know…it wasn't a no-strings, one-night-stand kind of deal for me. For one thing, I'm not that guy. That aside, every moment with you felt different from the beginning. More intense."

She swallowed, with difficulty. "For me, too. Hence the note. I panicked. I ran."

He pressed his lips together, looking sad.

"I'm so scared, Nate," she whispered, pressing her cheek against his chest again.

"Of course you are. I am, too. We'd be idiots if we weren't. We're going to be parents, and we're just now becoming a part of each other's lives. That's damned terrifying."

She couldn't comment.

He lifted her chin with one finger, urging her to meet his gaze. "I really do get it. I'm not asking you to pledge your life to me. It's way too soon for that, for both of us. I'm just asking for a chance. A new start. That's all I want."

"How? After all we've already been through?"

He kissed her gently, nipping at her lips. "How about something simple. I ask you for a date and you say yes?"

She laughed wryly, glancing down at her belly. "That's definitely doing things backward. I'm carrying your child, and we spend virtually every night together."

His lips twitched. "Yeah, I thought of that, too. But who says we have to do things like the rest of the world? Conformity is overrated."

He kissed her again, and she leaned into it, breathing him in, leaving her lips against his after the kiss.

Finally, he pulled away. "We're special. Don't you feel it, too?"

"Yes, but—" She bit her bottom lip and blinked, warring with herself, with all her mixed-up feelings. She peered up at him, wary. "I honestly don't know if I can let you see my scars. I don't even look at them if I can avoid it."

"Honey, there is no rush. I'm talking sweet, old-fashioned courtship, not hot sex."

She smirked. "Bummer."

"Well now—" he held up a hand "—that can be renegotiated at any time. Believe me."

"I was kidding. I'm an elephant, if you hadn't noticed."

He cupped her face in his hands. "All I've noticed is that you're my beautiful Erin. And we're having a baby."

"I'm not beautiful, though. That's what I keep

trying to tell you." Distress pooled tears in her eyes. He just didn't get it. "I'm scarred. Extensively. I've had a million surgeries, it seems. Skin grafts. Plastic surgery." She raised her shoulders, then let them drop in defeat. "There's nothing more they can do, and it's not pretty."

"Erin DeLuca. Every part of you that makes you the woman you are is beautiful to me. I couldn't care less about the scars."

She wanted to believe it, but...

"That's just because you haven't seen them."

"Not true. Once you know me better, you'll believe that. The point is, I don't have to see them. Until you're ready."

"What if I'm never ready?"

A look she couldn't quite name moved across his face. "We'll work through it."

A thick pause ensued.

"There's more, yes?" he urged.

She nodded. Gulped.

"Might as well lay it all out on the table."

Fear clutched at her. "Please understand—ugh, I shouldn't even ask that of you."

"It's okay. Whatever it is."

She trembled, knowing that once she said it, she couldn't take it back. But she had to say it. Do or die. "I feel...disloyal."

He tucked his chin. "To Kevin?"

She nodded again, hating that she had to voice this part of it at all. Nate deserved so much better.

"Because I want to take you out on a date?"

"No." She met his gaze directly. "Because I really, really want you to take me out on a date. And I want to keep sleeping in your arms like I have been. And whenever you touch me, all I want is more." She held up a hand. "Post-pregnancy, of course."

His lips twitched with amusement. "Of course."

"Is that wrong?" she finished, in a wavery whisper. "I swore I'd never feel a thing for any other man again. I feel like such a liar."

"Aw, honey." He pulled her back into an embrace. "It's difficult to be the survivor. But we can't control our feelings. Maybe…just maybe… Kevin would want to see you happy."

"But it breaks my heart that you'd feel like second place in any way. I want *you* to be happy, too."

"Then say yes. Being with you makes me happy. It's enough for now. Truly."

"Even when I stand here, pregnant with your baby, and tell you I feel disloyal to a boy I loved who's been…gone for almost twelve years?"

"Yes."

She took in a deep breath. "Well, then, go ahead."

"Go ahead?" he asked.

"You haven't actually asked me out yet."

"Oh. That. Thanks for the reminder." He readjusted his stance, preparing. "Erin DeLuca, would you please be my July Fourth date?"

She eased away enough to meet his gaze. "July Fourth? Don't you have to work?"

"I called in my VisionPlex and FogScreen experts." He smiled. "This next week I'll be working hellish, exhausting hours pulling the whole gig together, don't get me wrong. But on the day of the show? All I have to do is sit back and bask in a job well done. With you. If you agree, that is."

She angled her head to the side, her expression growing serious again. "No promises, okay? And we have to take things slowly. I'm skittish, Nate, and I'm...not whole. In so many ways."

"Whatever you need. I mean that."

"In that case, I'd love to be your date." She smiled cautiously up at him.

"Excellent." He kissed her forehead as though this kind of affection were second nature to him now, then went back to packing up his equipment. For a few moments, they enjoyed a comfortable silence. "You know, Brody thought you might want to kill him for accidentally spilling your secrets."

"Months ago? Probably." She twirled a lock of hair in her fingers. "But if he hadn't told you, I don't know that I ever could've."

"Really?"

"Yeah. The night of the Millstone fire, after it

had all hit me but before I met you, Brody assured me things would get better. I couldn't see how, and I asked him for help. So, it's on me." She hiked one shoulder. "I owe him."

"He'll be relieved to hear that."

"Nate, I have to tell you one more thing." She cut her gaze away, unsure if she could go on. She wasn't quite as brave as Brody yet.

"Tell me."

Could she? Yes. She had to. He deserved some consideration, too. She lowered her chin, regarding him through her lashes. "I've told you before, but it bears repeating. I didn't intend to get pregnant. You know that. You believe me, right?"

He nodded.

Her heart pounded so hard, the baby started to squirm in protest. "But, since it happened, you also have to know…really know, right here—" she pressed her palm to his chest, right over his heartbeat "—that I'm so glad the baby is yours. I am. I couldn't ask for a better father for my child. For a better man, period."

He searched her face for a long time, then reached over and tucked her hair behind her ear, running the backs of his fingers along her jawline before letting the caress drop away. "You know what? We're going to be okay, honey. No matter what happens between us."

"Are you sure?" she whispered.

"Sure enough for both of us. For all three of us," he amended, laying his palm on her belly. "That's plenty for now, yeah?"

She smiled, grateful. "Yeah."

Chapter Twelve

The alternative fireworks show was, naturally, a massive hit. Walt Hennessey took credit for the whole thing, but Nate had seen enough of his kind to anticipate that would happen. He didn't care. As long as the show made Erin happy, the rest didn't matter.

In addition to the whole town and residents from nearby towns, representatives from Denver's major media outlets had shown up. The positive press they'd receive for thinking environmentally about the fire danger would definitely give Troublesome Gulch a bigger pin on the Colorado map.

The fact that Nate had had a hand in making that happen swelled his heart with pride.

He sat on a blanket with Erin cradled against his chest. Brody and Faith had joined them, as had Lexy. Mr. Norwood accompanied Jason and a couple of his friends, and they sat just a few yards away.

Cagney was on duty—she always seemed to be on duty—but she stopped by to say hello, which they all enjoyed.

They'd indulged in fried chicken and biscuits from the Pinecone—grilled, skinless chicken skewers for Erin with fresh fruit—and now they simply basked in the aftermath, enjoying the music.

"You're a miracle worker, Nate," Faith said. She eyed Erin sitting comfortably in his arms. Pointedly. "And not just because that was, bar none, the coolest Fourth of July celebration the Gulch has ever seen, if you know what I'm saying, and I think you do."

"Let it go, Faith," Erin said softly.

Faith held up her hands. "I'm not pushing, Erin, except…it almost makes me cry to see you looking so happy. It's all I ever wanted for you. That's all." She mimed pulling a zipper over her lips.

To his great pleasure, Erin didn't protest. If anything, she snuggled closer. To him that said she was happy enough to not hide their burgeoning relationship from her friends. But he didn't want to read too much into anything at this point. He just wanted to enjoy every moment.

"I agree with Faith," Lexy said. "And, on that positive note, I have to go. I promised to cover part of the graveyard shift in dispatch."

"You work too damn much," Brody chastised.

She simply shrugged. "My work gives my life purpose. I love it. You know that."

"Wait, Lex, we'll walk you to the parking lot." Faith ran her palm against Brody's face. "We should go, too. I'm exhausted, and I have to work in the morning."

Brody immediately got to his feet and offered a hand to his wife. "What my babies want, my babies get."

Faith winked at Erin. "He's so trained, girl."

Everyone laughed.

After a round of goodbyes with the new friends he'd already come to treasure, Nate found himself blissfully alone with Erin. He slid his arms around her and laid his palms gently on her belly. Putting his lips close to her ear, he whispered, "I swear, I could hold you like this forever."

She squirmed languidly against him. "Man, I wish I weren't pregnant right now."

His body stirred. He nipped gently at her earlobe.

"Stop with the ear thing. You're driving me crazy."

"You know," he said, in a slow growl, "pregnant women *can*—"

"Not this pregnant woman. Sorry."

He chuckled softly. "Can't blame a guy for trying." He snuggled her in closer. "I won't lie, Erin. I want to make love to you so badly, it's painful."

"I want it, too. Just not yet. It'll be a while now."

He groaned. "I need a cold shower."

"Typical man, one-track mind," she said, in a teasing tone. She eased her way out of his embrace, despite his protestations, and started to gather up the trash from their picnic dinner. "We should probably go, too."

"Wait. I have something to tell you," Nate said.

Her hands stilled. After a moment, she glanced up.

"Don't look so scared. It's nothing awful. Well," he added ruefully, "nothing *too* awful."

"What?"

"I'm afraid the Walkers are descending. I held them at bay as long as I could."

Her eyes widened. "Your family?"

"Every last bossy, estrogen-packed one of them, and they will come bearing baby gifts. Be forewarned. You might want to rent a storage unit."

"Oh, God, I'm scared." She laid a hand at her throat, then laughed. "Then again, I can't wait. When?"

"Day after tomorrow. So, I've been meaning to

ask you, which hotel in town is best? My place is way too small for the four of them."

"Nate, they're family!"

"I know, but you've seen the condo. They won't be comfortable packed in like sardines."

She sat back on her knees, biting the corner of her lip. "What if they stay at my place? I have a guest room that'll sleep two, and my living room couch folds out. That'll sleep the other two." She shrugged. "It's not private, but it's better than a hotel. And if it's too awkward, two of them can take my bedroom and I'll stay at your place with you."

"Now, that sounds like a plan."

"Oh, you."

After a moment, he reached out and took her hand. "You'd really put my family up in your house?"

"Of course, silly," she said, softly. "They're sort of my family, too. Connected by the little one, of course."

It hit him right then, like a Louisville Slugger to the skull. He loved this woman.

Loved her. With every fiber of his being. Not because they'd created a baby together, either. He'd fallen headfirst in love with Erin DeLuca, simply because of who she was.

Gulping back the knowledge, he went for stern. "You will not play hostess. If you so much as lift a finger—"

"I won't. I'm way too exhausted these days."
She rubbed her tummy. "I honestly wonder if I'm
going to make it all the way to my due date."

"Not to worry. They'll wait on you hand and
foot—I'll make sure of that."

She laughed. "And I'll gladly let them. Call
them. Tonight. Now, if you have your cell phone."
She nearly bounced with excitement. "Tell them
they're welcome to stay with me, if they'd like.
And I can't wait to meet them."

He whistled low through his teeth. "You don't
know what you're in for, honey." He unclipped the
cell phone from his waistband. "But, okay, you
asked for it."

All the Walker siblings were on the tall side
and had Nate's dark hair and turquoise eyes, except
for Colette, a petite and surprisingly natural ash
blonde with a heart-shaped face and bright green
catlike eyes. All of them were stunning beauties,
at least in Erin's estimation.

Their arrival had been a flurry of chatter and
laughter, bear hugs and belly touches. Everyone
talked over each other, and no one lost track of any
conversation threads. Erin felt a little awed and
overwhelmed by all of it, but not necessarily in a
negative way. She wasn't used to big families, but
she found herself so grateful that her little son or

daughter would have aunts. And someday, maybe uncles and cousins, too.

After the initial onslaught, Flannery, Piper, Colette and Nate went to unload the SUV. Erin and Nate's mother, "call me LeAnn," sat in the Adirondack chairs sipping lemonade, with Finn snoring at their feet.

Despite her heartfelt desire to relax, tension hummed inside Erin, pulling her shoulders taut. She wanted them to like her, to approve. But there were things she needed to say, and she was determined not to lose her nerve.

"You have a lovely place, sweetheart," LeAnn said, in a casual tone, taking it all in. "It's no wonder my Nate didn't hesitate to move here."

This was it. Her chance. She cleared her throat. "Ms. Walker—"

"Ah—" the older woman held up a hand "—LeAnn, remember?"

"Right. Sorry." She smiled tightly. "Anyway...I just wanted to say...well, it's difficult."

"What's on your mind?"

Erin exhaled. "I honestly didn't mean to get your son tied up in this mess. I hope you know that. I even offered him an easy out."

LeAnn barked a laugh, then reached over and covered Erin's hand with her own. "I don't mean to laugh, but my Nate would never take an easy out."

"I've learned that since." Erin smiled. "Still, please, accept my most sincere apologies. I don't want you to think badly of me."

LeAnn turned and studied her. "Sweet child, let me tell you something. Any mother would want to see her child married and blissful before starting a family, that I won't lie about. But Nate has never done anything the easy or expected way." She shook her head. "I don't know the details of how this whole thing came about, and I don't need to. You're both grown adults. Just know that Nate has been happier since he moved to Troublesome Gulch than I've seen him in years, and mind you, he's a generally happy kid. That's saying something."

Erin nodded, amused to hear Nate referred to as a kid.

LeAnn leaned closer. "Listen here. You're the mother of my first grandchild. Do you know what that means?"

Erin swallowed, then shook her head jerkily.

"You're family, from here on out. Period. No inquisitions, no judgments, no nothing. It's the way we Walkers operate."

Erin breathed a sigh of relief. "I'm so…well, glad seems such an inadequate word." She shrugged. "I know Nate and I aren't your traditional parents, but we're both going to love this baby, and I'm so grateful he will have you and the girls as his family."

LeAnn quirked an eyebrow. "I don't want any more apology talk, hear? Family is family, no matter how it comes about. The girls and I are thrilled about the baby. And Nate?" She lifted her eyes heavenward. "Over the moon."

"He's an incredible guy."

"Yes, he is. And I take full credit."

"You should. I told him his mother should be proud of him that—" she gulped "—that first night we met."

LeAnn eyed Erin sidelong. "To hear you talk about my son, I just have to be nosy. Is it simply that you don't want the married life, sweetie? Not that it's any of my business, but believe me, I'd understand."

"It's not that." Erin sighed. "It's complicated."

"Well, there's time. Things have a way of working themselves out the way they should."

"Thank you, LeAnn. For being so…nonjudgmental. And for raising such an amazing man. I couldn't ask for a better man to be the father of my baby."

"You're absolutely right." LeAnn nailed her with an unwavering look, her tone light but pointed. "Keep that in mind when you're facing all these so-called complications, sweetheart. Okay?"

Erin dropped her gaze.

"Now, enough of my not-so-subtle hints that I'd like to see you and Nate together in a more permanent way." LeAnn laughed out loud. "To the nitty-gritty, and I'm sure Nate warned you I'd ask. I'm a registered nurse and a four-time mom myself—not the least bit squeamish. So? How's the pregnancy been so far? As Grandma-to-be, I want all the gory details."

The Walker women took time to rest and unpack, while Erin and Nate left to pick up food.

"How's it going so far?" Nate asked warily.

"Your family is amazing. I love them already." The deep yearning to be a part of them shocked Erin to her core. She hadn't wanted to be a part of a family this fervently since Kevin's.

Again with the guilt.

Nate smiled, turning into the pizza place. "That, they are. If it helps any, they love you, too. And this after only knowing you for a couple hours. But I could've predicted that."

Erin demurred. "It's only because I'm carrying their grandchild-slash-niece or nephew. Otherwise I'd just be one woman in a long line of them, I'm sure."

"I'm not going to waste time being offended by that last comment." Nate huffed. "When are you going to give yourself a little credit?"

She crinkled her nose. "I'm not sure I deserve it."

Their pizzas were probably ready and waiting,

but Nate killed the ignition and angled to face her. "You and Brody." He shook his head sadly. "Don't tell me you blame yourself for the prom night accident, too?"

"No, not really. But…there's Kevin. Sorry. Plus, I feel like I roped you into this makeshift family thing, and you're just too nice to say so. It's not a good feeling."

A beat passed.

"How am I going to get through to you?"

"What do you mean?"

"I wouldn't want to be having a child with any other woman, Erin. I don't want any other woman in my life. Can't you see what you've come to mean to me?"

She studied him quizzically, then reached out to hold his hand.

"I could fall in love with you in a split second," he said, in a silky-rough tone. "Lord knows, I'm half-crazy in love with you already."

Her chest warmed, but she brushed him off. He didn't know what he was saying. "Don't be silly."

"I'm not. I'm holding back in deference to you—period. But I think you're the most amazing, beautiful, complicated, intriguing woman I've ever come across, and I want to go on record right this minute saying, I'm ready and waiting whenever you're ready."

"And waiting?"

He pulled her toward him. "Honey, you won't have to wait for a second. All you have to do is say the word."

"Nate," she said, on an exhale.

"It's true."

Her throat squeezed. "Kiss me. I need you to kiss me."

He hesitated for only a second before maneuvering closer to her. Cradling her face in his hands, he kissed her gently, butterfly kisses.

"Kiss me like you mean it, Nate." She lowered her tone to a purr. "I know you can. I know I'm gross and huge and pregnant, but kiss me like you want me."

His gaze deepened, and he released a half laugh, half groan. "You're neither gross nor huge, although I'll concede, you *are* pregnant. And, just FYI, I *do* want you." He threaded his fingers into the back of her hair and did as she asked, exploring her mouth with his own, trailing kisses down her neck and across her collarbone.

"Why does this feel so good?"

"Because it's right," he said, nibbling at her bottom lip. "Because it's time you stopped fighting me so hard."

She kissed him this time, throwing every bit of her pent-up sexual tension into the kiss. When they broke apart, they both breathed heavily. "I'm not fighting you, Nate. I'm scared."

"I know, babe."

She rested her head on his shoulder. "You're so good to me."

"Then let me be."

A protest lit on her lips. She bit it back. "We should get the pizzas."

"I don't want to leave you."

She sighed. "I don't want you to leave me."

He pulled her closer. "Screw it. We can let my family starve. I don't mind."

She laughed, the intense moment broken. "Oh, be quiet. They're my guests. Our guests. I won't let them starve in my own house."

He released a put-upon sigh. "Fine, fine. Pizzas it is." He pulled away, but kept hold of her hand. "Know this. I want you, Erin. You and our baby. I'm not going to lie about it anymore."

She searched his eyes for several long moments, then squeezed his hand. "I'm working on it, Nate, but I'm not quite ready. And I don't know what to do to get ready. You deserve better than always having to wait."

"I don't want better. Better doesn't exist. I want you. Besides—" he pulled away before she could protest "—I'm more than willing to bide my time. You, sweet one, are more than worth the wait."

Chapter Thirteen

For two days straight, Erin and Nate focused solely on his family. They showed them around town, introduced them to their friends. Mostly, though, they spent time at her house just talking and laughing, getting to know each other. None of them let Erin do a single task in her supposed capacity of hostess.

Piper, Erin quickly learned, was an avid—okay, obsessed—knitter. No matter where they went, the woman always had her needles clickity-clacking. She'd finished a veritable motherlode of absolutely darling booties and caps and sweaters for the baby already, in every color of the rainbow, and she showed no signs of letting up.

But she was running low on yarn.

Catastrophe for a knitting addict like her.

The third day, Erin woke up exhausted, her back aching and her head pounding. She didn't want to spoil the Walkers' visit, so she begged off a planned road trip into Denver, assuring them she just needed to catch up on sleep and she'd be good as new when they returned that evening. She equipped Nate with the addresses of and directions to three great knitting shops in the metro area—The Recycled Lamb, Showers of Flowers and Simplicity—then shuffled the whole family out the door, demanding they have enough fun to share with her later.

Not thirty minutes after they'd left, she'd fallen into a fitful, restless sleep.

A few hours into her nap, she became half-aware of a sense that someone was standing in her room, right at the end of her bed. Finn hadn't roused to attack an intruder—a good sign. She felt so groggy, she didn't have the sense to feel afraid.

Still, she opened her eyes to see who was there, more out of curiosity than anything.

She sucked a breath.

"K-Kevin?" Her heart hammered in her chest.

No. Couldn't be.

Kevin was dead.

He'd been gone for more than ten years.

A hallucination.

She squeezed her eyes closed, then opened them again, slowly.

He still stood there. Incongruous in the bedroom of her adult home, but on the other hand, so normal. Close, but distant. He wore his Troublesome Gulch letter jacket and looked just as he always had. Sweet, alive, loving.

Young.

It had to be a dream or a hallucination.

She'd aged. He hadn't.

He looked just as he had before he'd died.

Still, she wanted him there.

Terrified he'd disappear without warning, she eased into a sitting position slowly. "Kevin?" she whispered.

Why wasn't he talking?

"Say something," she demanded, urgency seizing her in a way it never had before. Tears filled her eyes and spilled over. "Please say something to me."

Nothing. But he reached out a hand.

She edged to the end of the bed and sat back on her knees, sobbing full force. She reached toward his hand, but felt...nothing. "Oh, God. Kev, why are you here now? When you're not *really* here? Why?"

"Let me go," she heard him whisper.

She reeled back as though she'd been punched. Had she imagined those words?

"Let me go," she heard again.

"How?" She wadded fistfuls of the quilt in her hands. "Tell me how, Kevin, and I will. I know I need to. It's been so long, and I haven't really been living, but you don't get it. You were the love of my life."

"I get it."

She gulped several times. "I have so much I want to say to you. So much I never got to say. I feel angry and sad and cheated."

"Say it."

"But you're not real!" she yelled in frustration, then felt an immediate stab of remorse. "I mean, you're real in here." She touched her chest, just over her heart. "I will always love you. But you're not real on this earth anymore. I can't be with you."

He didn't move, didn't speak, just smiled.

Everything about him seemed serene.

In contrast, she sobbed harder, and the baby kicked, pulling her into her current reality. She laid her palm against her belly, then blinked up at the spectre of the young man she'd thought she would spend the rest of her life with. Surely he couldn't miss the huge bulge.

"I'm having a baby, Kev." She swallowed

thickly. This felt so weird. "With a great guy. Nate. You'd like him, I think."

He smiled. Nodded. "I like him."

"God, Kev, I can't believe I'm saying this to you, but I think I'm in love with him. No—" She held out a hand, knowing she couldn't lie anymore. Not to herself, and definitely not to Kevin. "I am in love with him."

He nodded.

"I'm so sorry," she whispered, her words wavering. "I never meant to betray you."

"There's no betrayal."

"Do you hate me?" she pleaded, through ever-increasing sobs.

"I love you," he said, simply.

The pain lanced through her. "I love you, too. I always will. But I love Nate, too. And I don't know what to do. C-can you understand that?"

"Yes. So, let me go. Be happy. Please…"

She jammed shaky fingers into her hair, frustrated for the unfairness of it all. "But I was supposed to have your baby, Kevin."

"No. You weren't."

Her eyes bugged. What? How could he say that?

"D-don't you remember our baby?"

"Of course I do. You don't understand. There's a grand plan." He paused. "I'm with her. Our baby. She was for *me*. Not you."

"Oh, God," Erin keened, clutching at the front of her T-shirt.

"She's beautiful. Happy, too. Don't worry about us." He smiled, gesturing toward her belly. "You're supposed to have *this* baby. With Nate. Please, Er-bear, let us go. It's time."

He started to fade, and panic set in.

"Wait!" she yelled, scrambling to her knees. "What if I can't, Kev? I—I don't know how—"

"You know," he said, with quiet confidence. "It's inside you. Stop hiding." He faded further.

"Kevin!" she sobbed. "Kevin, please, wait!"

But he didn't.

The last vision she had was of him blowing her a kiss that she actually felt like small wings against her cheek.

A baby girl. She'd lost a baby girl. Bereft, she couldn't even revel in a sense of peace that the little angel was with her daddy in heaven, loved and cared for.

She fell onto her side, curled protectively around the baby in her womb and wept. She wept until she didn't have a drop of moisture left in her body, it seemed, then fell into a deadweight, dreamless sleep.

When she jolted awake, late-afternoon sunshine slanted through her windows. Strangely rejuvenated, she glanced around the room—just as it had been when she'd fallen asleep that morning.

Had the whole thing been a dream?

It had to have been.

The fetus she'd lost was too small to discern gender—they'd told her that at the hospital. A girl? How could anyone know?

But, it had felt so real.

And everything she'd said to Kevin felt real, too, she realized, a sort of zen calm settling over her. She loved Nate. She wanted to be whole for him, to be with him, and finally, she had an idea of what she needed to do to gain some closure.

Time to stop hiding, and this would be step one.

After showering quickly, she dressed, fed Finn, and scribbled a note for Nate.

Running errands, back soon. Don't worry.

She hesitated, then added, *Love, Erin.*

The thirty-mile drive to nearby White Peaks didn't take her too long. Kevin's parents had moved there after the prom night accident that stole their only son. They couldn't face living in Troublesome Gulch without him, and she could hardly blame them.

She arrived at their cedar-sided bungalow right about 7:00 p.m., glad they'd be done with dinner. God knew, she wouldn't be able to swallow a single bite if they offered her a meal.

Anxiety rose and fell within her, like a runaway cart on a roller coaster. She hadn't spoken to Kevin's parents since last Christmas. Sadly, after years of family-like contact, it had come to that…a phone call each Christmas, probably to avoid pain on both sides. And yet, she realized she really wanted them to know about her baby. More than that, to *know* her baby. Like her, Kevin had been an only child. Their dreams of being grandparents had died on prom night, along with their son.

None of it was fair.

Heart in her throat, she pressed the doorbell and stepped back, listening to the chimes. Through the door, she could hear the television. When footsteps approached, she resisted the insane urge to bolt, forget the whole ridiculous idea. Since when had she been afraid of Kevin's parents?

The door swung open, and there stood Kevin's lovely mom, PJ, an expectant smile on her face. Her expression brightened even more.

"My goodness, Erin!" She started to step forward for a hug, then her gaze dropped to Erin's belly. Tremulous fingers raised to her lips, tears rose to her eyes, and she whispered, "Oh, honey."

"I wanted you to know," Erin blurted, her words watery and shaky. "I should've come much sooner. Please forgive me."

"Come here." The two women dissolved into tears, hugging and rocking each other on the front porch.

"I loved Kevin," Erin said, her words muffled against his mother's shoulder. "I hope you know that."

"Of course you did, honey." She pulled back, laying her palms on Erin's belly. "But you have to move on. We all do. I've worried for so long that you never would, but look at you now."

"Yeah. Big and fat."

"Beautiful." PJ laughed through her tears. "He'd be so happy for you, honey. He would. I'm happier for you than I can even say. When are you due?"

"About three weeks."

PJ put her arm around Erin's shoulders and ushered her in. "I can't tell you how pleased I am that you came. Better late than never, they say. Marcus!" she called out. "Erin's here!"

"Our Erin?" he said, and she could hear the excitement, the welcome, in his tone, and it warmed her. She recognized the sound of the newspaper being set aside, and of the footrest of his favorite green recliner clicking down. Familiar things.

The house smelled of lemon furniture polish and pine, as their houses always had, even though this one was relatively new. Some things carried though a life, like a safety line to normalcy.

"Yes," PJ called to her husband, "and with a big surprise."

Marcus Jennings, looking so much the way Erin had always imagined Kevin would in their later days, rounded the corner and stopped dead, taking in the sight. His eyes grew suspiciously bright, and his chin quivered. He opened his arms wide. "Erin DeLuca. You make an absolutely beautiful mama, like we always knew you would. Come here, little one."

Feeling like a teenager again, she cried in Marcus's arms, but the tears cleansed her soul this time rather than weighing on it. "I'm having a baby," she said, unnecessarily.

Everyone laughed.

"Come." He cradled her against him as though she were a precious thing. "Sit down and tell us all about it. This is a happy day. A happy day, indeed."

With the ice broken, their conversation came as easily as it always had prior to the tragedy. She didn't go into all the embarrassing details, but she did tell them about Nate and his family, about the baby and her pregnancy.

Finally, she worked up the urge to admit the dream she'd had about Kevin, and what he'd said about the baby granddaughter they'd lost. Of course, no one had known she and Kevin were expecting on prom night, but they all found out in the aftermath. By then, it was the least of anyone's worries.

PJ tucked her feet beneath her on the couch as she listened to the story of Erin's "Kevin dream." "I'm not surprised. Kevin comes to me on a pretty regular basis. Whenever I need him."

Erin gaped, unable to speak for a moment. "Why hasn't he come to me before?"

PJ smiled, looking so much like Kevin—at peace and serene. "You weren't ready. Now you are. You're prepared to heal and move on. Thank the Lord."

Erin pondered this, nodding. It really had been a gift, seeing Kevin that way.

"I knew about the baby girl, too."

Erin peered curiously at PJ. "How?"

"Kevin told me. He calls her Phoenix."

A melancholy overtook Erin, but she shook it off. This wasn't a time to dwell in the past. She looked up at the two people she'd considered a second family since high school. "I wanted to tell you both about the baby…and about Nate. I love him so much."

"You didn't have to wait so long," Marcus chided.

She nodded, biting her lip. "I didn't know how much I needed to tell you until Kevin came to my room. Before that, I'd been floundering. Confused. I couldn't figure out what I needed."

"He's watched over you this whole time, honey. Every step, and he'll continue to do so," PJ said. "But it's about time you lived your life. Please believe Kevin would've wanted that for you—love, life, family. Take advantage of the chance he lost."

"I will."

"You're going to be such a good mom."

She grimaced. "I'm glad you think so. It's terrifying."

PJ laughed. "You'll get the hang of it. We all do. That's just part of it."

"Will you bring the baby by?" Marcus asked, in a far-off, wistful tone, his fists in a knot on his lap.

"That's the thing." She looked from one to the other, then leaned forward and took their hands into hers. "Why I came, really." She paused.

"What is it, sweetheart?" PJ asked.

Erin garnered her courage. "I want you to be a part of this baby's life. A big part. I know you won't be his or her real grandparents, but I consider you my family and always will."

"The feeling's mutual."

"The way I figure it, a child can't have too many great adults in his life, you know?" She watched them nod, preparing for her next words. "So, please, will you be my baby's godparents? Will you take an active role in his or her life? If it's not too much to ask, that is," she added shyly. "Mom and Dad live farther away now, and Nate's family is from Las Vegas. Nate travels extensively for his business, and I'm eventually going back to those twenty-four hour shifts, too. He or she will need a loving place to stay."

PJ had begun crying silently.

"As far as I'm concerned, he can have Grandma and Grandpa DeLuca, Grandma Walker and Nana and Papa Jennings."

PJ sniffed. "Oh, Erin. We'd love nothing more. Such a gift in all our lives, this child. And you. Thank you, sweetheart. Thank you."

Marcus swallowed convulsively, reining in his emotions. "Is Nate okay with our involvement?"

She squeezed their hands one final time and released them, smiling. "I haven't discussed it with him, but I know him well enough to say yes. Definitely. He's an amazing, selfless man. You'll love him."

"If he loves you, I can't see how we wouldn't." Marcus looked at his wife, grinning. "Time to go baby shopping, Mother. We've got some work to do, turning that spare room into a nice nursery and playroom for our godchild."

"Yes." PJ gulped back tears and gratitude, her hands clasped at her chest. "And I can't wait. Three weeks, goodness, it seems a lifetime now."

Erin navigated the quickly darkening roads with extra care, despite her urgency to get home. A lightness of being had overtaken her; she hadn't felt this free since high school. She could hardly wait to tell Nate everything. That she loved him—heart, mind, body and soul. She wanted to tell him about Kevin coming to her in a dream, about visiting Kevin's parents, about breaking through her own self-imprisonment and finally—*finally*—being ready to move forward.

With him. The man she adored.

Her back throbbed even more from all the time spent in the car, but she was flying so high on emotion, she didn't even care.

Thoughts of the new life that awaited her raced through her brain as the miles rolled beneath her tires. The closer she got, the more excited she became.

Just on the outskirts of Troublesome Gulch proper, a sudden, blinding pain shot through her abdomen, and she jerked the wheel. By the time she'd identified it as a labor pain, everything moved in slow motion, and she realized it was too late to regain control of the careening car. As a seasoned engineer, she knew this.

Still, she had to try.

She gripped the wheel as the car screeched toward the empty oncoming lines and the mountain that flanked them. She couldn't hit that. Overcorrecting, she turned the car, tires squealing to the other side where it dipped off the edge of the road into a ditch.

She held her breath and prayed though the jolting and crunching, the sounds of breaking glass around her, until finally the vehicle came to rest on its side.

Eerie silence filled the car.

She'd struck her head hard on the driver's side window, and it took her several moments to shake off confusion, to get her bearings. A second blinding labor pain helped the process along. She reached up to touch the side of her head and pulled away bloody fingers. So, what now?

She fought back panic, knowing she could handle herself in an emergency like this. She did it for a living, for God's sake.

First step, get help.

Glancing around, she caught sight of her purse splayed on the splintered passenger side window currently pressed against the gouged earth. She flailed for it, but it was just out of reach.

Fear set in, icy and raw. She struggled to squelch it. No matter what, she was not going to give birth to her baby in a crashed car with no one around. Scared or not, she absolutely *had* to keep her wits about her.

Carefully loosening her seat belt without actually unlatching it, since she didn't want to fall, she managed enough slack to hook the strap of her purse with her fingertips, wrenching her shoulder in the process. Cringing against the new pain, she pulled the purse toward her, then dug inside for her cell phone. Relieved to have a signal, she pressed in 9-1-1 with shaky, bloody fingers.

"Troublesome Gulch 9-1-1, what is your emergency?"

"Lex?" she said, through gritted teeth and the onslaught of another contraction.

"Erin?"

Consumed in the pain, she couldn't speak.

"Erin! What's wrong?"

The agony eased, and she sucked a breath. "I, uh, had a little accident."

"What do you mean?" her normally calm, cool and in-charge friend asked, clearly alarmed.

"I mean my car's in a ditch on it's side, and I'm in it. Dangling from my seat belt. I hit my head."

"Is the baby okay? What are you doing out driving, for God's sake? You could've called any one of us."

"I had something I needed to do. Alone. But now I need help." Her voice shook. "Please tell me Brody is working a rig tonight."

"He is. And so is your crew at Station Eight."

"Thank God. Can you send them? All of them?" She provided her exact location.

"Stay on the phone with me, understand?"

Another contraction hit, and Erin couldn't speak. They seemed to be hitting closer together than they should be at this point.

"Erin? Erin?"

"I'm here. Hurry," she said, her voice choking.

"Everyone's going code three."

"Wait. One other thing, Lex."

"Yeah?"

"I'm in labor."

"Oh, God. Are you bleeding?"

It was the first time Erin had ever heard Lexy lose her cool in an emergency. She peered down. "Just from my head. It's okay. The baby's okay, I think. He or she just wants out. Soon. Please, please hurry."

"You know we will." She covered her mic and said something to her partner. "Dane has already dispatched, and they know who their patient is."

"Tell them to drive carefully."

"Hang in there, doll face, okay? I am right here with you and I'm going nowhere."

"Mmm-hmm." She sucked a breath and held it through another fierce contraction. When it ended, she said, "Lex? I'm scared. The contractions are too close together."

"I'm right here, hon. It's going to be fine."

"Can you call my parents?"

"Dane's on it."

"Tell them—"

"I know what to tell them. I have the phone tree."

"Cagney's my coach."

"I know, sweetie. Stop worrying. Let us worry. You just try to relax so your baby can, too. Remember your breathing, okay?"

"Okay." She gulped back her rising panic. "Can you also call Kevin's parents?"

A pause. "Really?"

"It's a long story for later, but yes."

"Done." Erin could hear Lexy's fingers typing lightning fast. "How painful are the contractions?"

"They suck." Erin tried to laugh. "Lex, can you do one more thing for me?"

"Anything."

"Can you call Nate? He should be at my house, but use his cell phone, just in case."

Lexy blew out a long breath. "I was hoping you'd say that. Of course."

"Tell him—" she gulped "—tell him I love him."

Lexy's tone softened. "You can do that when you see him. Okay? You're going to be just fine."

"Yes."

"Did you lose consciousness when you hit your head?"

"No. At least, I don't think so. But I'm bleeding."

"Right. Listen, you know how head wounds bleed. You're going to be perfect, Erin," Lexy assured her, all her normal confidence regained. "And, hey, you're going to be a mom."

"Yeah, wow, huh?" Erin focused on her breathing, listening as the sirens moved closer. "I always wanted to be a mom," she said, sniffling a bit.

"Funny how things work out, isn't it? Stick with me, sweetheart. The cavalry's almost there."

Chapter Fourteen

Nate burst through the doors of High Country Medical Center's Emergency Department, still unable to feel his extremities. His lips were numb, his brain buzzed. Fear nearly blinded him. His mom and sisters flanked him as he whipped a glance this way and that. He knew she'd come in by ambulance. "Mom?"

"Stay right here."

Flannery, Colette and Piper surrounded him while their mother strode purposefully to the desk and calmly explained their situation to the charge nurse. Thank God for Mom.

Nate had always heard that certain phone calls could cut ten years off a person's life in an instant, but he hadn't believed it until now. If he lost Erin—

"Damn it, I never should've left her today." He clenched his fists. "She's been saying for a week that she didn't feel like she'd make it to her due date."

"She's going to be okay, Nate," Flannery said.

"I can't lose her, Flan." He searched his older sister's face, gulping back his surging emotions. "Or the baby. I love them so much."

"We love them, too," Piper said. "*Nothing* bad is going to happen. I just know."

His sisters wrapped him in a hug.

His mom returned, all efficiency, no stress. "Labor and Delivery. Fifth floor. Come on."

He grasped his mother's arm. "Did they say how she was doing?"

"Of course not. We're going to find out."

The five of them rushed to the bank of elevators, and Colette pushed the button. They stared up at the display as all six elevators took their sweet time descending to the lobby floor—Murphy's Law.

"Come on, come on," Nate snapped, feeling as if he might explode.

His mother faced him, grasping both of his biceps to give him a little shake. "Nathaniel Walker, take a deep breath and pull yourself together this minute. The woman you love is about to give birth to your child. My grandchild. You need to be strong for her, understand?"

"I am." *Deep breath.* "I will."

Ding!

They all whipped toward the doors until they saw the ones with the indicator light glowing over them. In a pack, they pushed their way into the empty car before the doors had completely opened.

Again, Colette pushed the button for the fifth floor. Repeatedly. After an eternity, the doors eased shut, and the car began to ascend. When the doors opened onto floor five, Nate saw Brody and Faith pacing in front of the nurses' station. Nate couldn't read his friends' faces. Brody turned to the nurse. "Here. This is the baby's father."

"How is she?" Nate demanded.

Brody clasped a palm on his shoulder. "She's fine. Good. She has a slight concussion and a few stitches in her head, but labor's going well. That's what matters at this point. Not the head."

Nate sagged with relief. "I want to see her."

"Of course," Faith said, taking his hand. "Come on. She's in room twelve."

She ushered him forward a few steps, then he whipped back. "Mom?"

"Go, son. Your sisters and I will be in the waiting room whenever you need us."

He nodded.

At the door he hesitated. "Listen," he told Faith, expelling a breath. "I'm sure you know Cagney's her birth coach."

"Yes. But I know she wants to see you. She's been asking for you constantly." She tried to pull him in.

He held her arm. "Wait. I haven't seen her burn scars, and I'm not sure she wants me to during the birthing. I promised her I'd wait until she's ready. Can you go in first? Tell her I'm here and just… make sure?"

Faith smiled. "Of course, sweetie."

He flicked his hands to hurry Faith along.

She'd only been in the room for a moment before she emerged with a smile on her face. "Come on in, Daddy."

His eyes widened. "Already?"

"No, no. You haven't missed anything."

He nodded. Digging down deep for some inner calm, he entered the room. Erin was on the bed, all covered up. The side of her head was swollen and bruised, a bandage covering what was surely the stitches. His heart clenched. "Honey."

She glanced over, tears rushing to her eyes. "Come here." She held out her arms. "I'm so sorry. I didn't mean to scare you. I'm okay, really."

He reached her bedside in two long strides, bending down to cup the uninjured side of her face and kiss her deeply. "I'm so glad you're not—You really *are* okay, right?"

She nodded. "They gave me Tylenol for the head. Oh, and an epidural. Let me say, I've never been so happy to see such a frighteningly long needle in my life."

He gritted his teeth, warring between the need to be there for her completely and the need to apologize. "I should've been there with you."

"You didn't know. How could you? *I* didn't even know."

Cagney hovered uncertainly on the other side of the bed. "Hey, listen." She aimed a thumb over her shoulder. "I can leave if you'd like, Erin. Now that Nate's here."

"No." Erin held tightly to Nate's hand, but reached out for her friend's, too. She beseeched Nate. "I want you to stay, Nate, like I told Faith. I have so much to tell you—"

"Later."

"Yes. Anyway, I hadn't planned it this way, but I guess this will be the great unveiling of my hideous scars—"

"I don't care about your scars."

"I know." She gulped. "But I do. I'm scared out of my mind." She flashed a grateful smile at Cagney. "So, on that note, is it okay if Cagney stays for the birth, too? For moral support?"

With his elbows resting on the side bars of the gurney, Nate smiled tenderly. "You can have absolutely anyone you want here, love. Of course it's okay if Cagney stays. She's your birth coach. I'm just the hapless father."

They all laughed.

"I'm just going to dash out and update the crowd, okay?" Cagney said, clearly psyched that she would still be able to witness the birth.

"Hurry back," Erin said.

Once they were alone, Erin took both of Nate's hands into her own. "I didn't expect this to happen so soon. My parents are on the way, but it'll be a while. I told them all about you," she rushed to add. "I'm sorry it wasn't until now. I thought I had more time."

"It's okay."

"Also, this is harder to explain, but Kevin's parents are on the way."

He peered down at her curiously.

"It's part of the long story for later, and I hope my instincts were correct. I asked them to be the baby's godparents."

"Oh, honey."

"Please understand. They lost their only son, Nate, and any chance of being grandparents. I just thought—"

"Baby, stop. It's perfect."

"Really?"

He squeezed her hand. "And truly. You're the most giving person I've ever met. I expect they were thrilled?"

"Beyond," she whispered. "I told them you'd support the decision. I told them—listen, this is one part of the long story that I can't wait to tell you. I don't want to."

He opened his mouth to speak.

"Wait. Let me get this out before another contraction hits. They're not excruciating now, but I can still feel them."

He inclined his head.

"Nate Walker, I'm in love with you. Completely. Totally. I love you more than anything."

"Erin," he whispered, in wonder.

"It took a weird dream and a long-overdue visit to make me realize how much, but I'm sure. And before this all gets ugly, I have something I want to ask you."

"Anything."

She searched his eyes. "Will you marry me?"

He barked out a shocked laugh, but warmth ran all through him. "Hey, isn't that supposed to be my line?"

"I didn't mean to steal your thunder. I just can't go through this whole birth thing not knowing. Besides, who says we have to do things like the rest of the world? Conformity is overrated." She smiled. "A really smart guy told me that once."

His heart expanded more than he ever thought possible. "Are you sure?"

"I've never been more sure of anything in my life. It's not like we've done anything the normal way from the very beginning, so why start now?" She held up a hand, pausing through a contraction, then expelled a breath once it had eased. "But, the bottom line is, I haven't truly lived for twelve years, Nate. Then you came into my life and filled up all the empty spaces in my heart. Kevin will always have a place there—"

"As he should."

"Yes," she whispered in a fervent tone, "but I love *you*. I see it now, so clearly. You're the man I'm supposed to be with, and our baby is the one fate intended me to deliver and raise." She shook her head. "I don't want to do it without you."

"Aw, Erin—"

"Look, I'm sorry I didn't think to get you a ring for the proposal. I was too busy crashing my car, getting a concussion and going into preterm labor. I hope that's not a deal breaker."

He chuckled. "That's where I draw the line."

She inhaled. "You're saying no?"

"Of course not. But I will get *you* the ring."

Her eyes widened. "Does that mean—?"

"Yes. One hundred percent. Because I can't imagine spending my life without you, either." He leaned down and kissed her tenderly on the lips. "I love you, Erin DeLuca. And I'd love to be your husband more than anything in this world."

Tears filled her eyes and rolled down into her ears. "Yay, me. I'm going to be a mommy and score the man of my dreams. I rule."

Cagney returned, glancing from Nate to Erin, then back. "What's going on?"

Nate gave her a wry smile. "Erin proposed to me."

"And he said yes!"

Reserved, stoic Cagney started sniffling. "I'm so, so happy for both of you. It's absolutely perfect." She rounded the bed and wrapped Nate in a bear hug, then leaned down and kissed Erin on the cheek. "You done good, kid."

"It's not over yet." She grimaced. "There's still this delivery thing to contend with."

As if on cue, the nurse whisked in. "Let's give you another check, honey. See how close you are."

Fear paled Erin's complexion. "Nate?"

He leaned closer to her face. "I'm going to look right here, into your beautiful eyes. Okay? There's no need for you to feel like a specimen on a table. When you're ready for me to look, you tell me."

"Okay."

The nurse did her thing, then pulled off her

gloves, dropping them into a nearby trash bin. "Miss Erin, it's time for you to have this baby."

"Really?" Erin's voice shook with nerves.

"Really." She raised her brows at Nate. "Time for you to get gowned and gloved, Daddy, if you're planning to stick around."

"He is," Erin insisted.

"Okay," Nate said, nervous, too, but more excited than anything. He started to follow the nurse.

"Wait." Erin grabbed his hand.

He turned to her.

She blinked twice, the trepidation clear in her eyes. "I want you to see them first. The scars."

He cocked his head. "Honey, look, there's plenty of time for that later. You don't have to do this now."

"Yes, I do. Because I want you to see our baby come into this world, and you won't be able to if you aren't allowed to look at my body. Please."

"They're not as bad as you think, Er," Cagney said, in her kind, reassuring tone.

Erin smiled at her friend. "Will you pull the blanket down, Cag?"

Cagney did so, then moved discreetly to the other side of the birthing room to give them privacy.

Erin squeezed her eyes shut. "Okay. Just do it."

With careful, gentle fingers, Nate raised the hospital gown. Erin's burn-scarred flesh ran from just beneath her full breasts all the way down to her pelvis. Extensive, sure, but all he saw was beauty.

He saw strength.

He saw a survivor.

He smoothed his palms gently over her body, then leaned down and kissed her, just over the baby.

"Well?" she choked out, eyes still clamped shut.

"Do you want to know what I see?"

She bit the corner of her bottom lip, hesitating. Then eased her eyes open and nodded.

He lowered the gown over her again. "I see a body so beautiful, so capable, that it carried our baby from conception until now. I see the woman I love. I see the pain of your past, sweet girl, but mostly I see our future." He paused. "These scars?" He shrugged. "They're nothing." He flicked his hand to the side. "The point is, look— we accidentally made a baby together, and the sky didn't fall. I've seen your scars, and the sky didn't fall. Best of all, we fell in love with each other, and now, Erin, the sky can never fall on us again."

"Nate," she gulped out.

"Enough of that." He clapped his hands together once, smoothing them palm to palm. "What do you say I get suited up so we can meet our baby?"

"Yes." She nodded happily. "Yes."

* * *

It took an hour and a half of pushing before their healthy baby boy emerged, red and squinty-eyed and squalling, into the world. All of them cried, including Cagney, the nurse and Dr. Kipfer, as Nate cut the cord.

Cagney left shortly thereafter to inform the crowd.

The little guy weighed in at just over six pounds, healthy, with all ten fingers and all ten toes, just like they'd prayed for. After he'd been cleaned up and swaddled in a soft, white receiving blanket, Dr. Kipfer handed him over to Nate with a wide smile. "Why don't you introduce him to his mother?"

Erin watched as Nate stared down at the wrinkly little bald-headed human he held. "What do you think?"

"I think he's the most beautiful thing I've ever seen. Next to his mother, that is."

"Bring him here."

He carried him over and placed him gently on her chest. Her heart squeezed.

"Say hello to your son."

"Oh, my God." Erin studied him in wonder. "He's perfect, Nate."

Nate lowered the side bars and perched next to her, cradling her shoulders as they admired their child. He had her nose and chin, Nate's gorgeous eyes. And as a pleasant and quite amusing surprise, he had Colette's ash blond hair, though not much of it.

"I have a great idea," Nate said.

She peered up at him. "What's that?"

"Let's name him Kevin Jennings DeLuca Walker."

Wide-eyed, Erin studied Nate's face, scarcely believing the immensity of her love for this man. It took her several moments before she could speak. "You're the most selfless person I know, Nate Walker. But I have a better idea."

"Lay it on me."

"He looks like a Nathaniel Kevin Deluca Walker to me. If that's okay with you." She peered into her son's squinchy little elfin face. "Frankly, I think it sounds just perfect."

Nate's voice came out husky, "Little Nate Junior, huh?"

"Is it okay?"

"Are you kidding?"

They laughed, and then Nate took hold of her chin. "I will love you, Erin DeLuca, and all of our children until the day I die. That's a promise."

"And I will never make you feel like second place again," she whispered. "Because, you're not. You're the man I was meant to spend my life with. It just took me a while to catch on. Deal?"

He kissed her nose. "Deal."

"Now that we've settled all that, how about we introduce the little man here to his friends and family before he knows what hit him?" She rolled her eyes. "If we don't open the floodgates soon they may riot, and we'll never hear the end of it."

A few minutes later, the room filled. Her parents, his mom and sisters—all of whom seemed to be getting on like old friends. Marcus and PJ Jennings, overcome with emotion for having been included. Brody, Faith, Jason—even Mr. Norwood. Cagney, of course, and Lexy, who'd just gotten off duty.

Family.

With Nate by her side and her healthy baby being passed from one person who loved him to another, Erin finally felt whole again.

She closed her eyes, at peace.

Just…being in the moment.

* * * * *

SPECIAL EDITION
Life, Love and Family

*These contemporary romances will strike
a chord with you as heroines juggle life
and relationships on their way to true love.*

New York Times *bestselling author*
Linda Lael Miller
*brings you a BRAND-NEW contemporary story
featuring her fan-favorite McKettrick family.*

Meg McKettrick is surprised to be reunited
with her high school flame, Brad O'Ballivan. After enjoying a career as a country-
and-western singer, Brad aches for a home
and family…and seeing Meg again makes
him realize he still loves her. But their pride
manages to interfere with love…until an
unexpected matchmaker gets involved.

*Turn the page for a sneak preview of
THE McKETTRICK WAY
by Linda Lael Miller
On sale November 20,
wherever books are sold.*

Brad shoved the truck into gear and drove to the bottom of the hill, where the road forked. Turn left, and he'd be home in five minutes. Turn right, and he was headed for Indian Rock.

He had no damn business going to Indian Rock.

He had nothing to say to Meg McKettrick, and if he never set eyes on the woman again, it would be two weeks too soon.

He turned right.

He couldn't have said why.

He just drove straight to the Dixie Dog Drive-In.

Back in the day, he and Meg used to meet at the

Dixie Dog, by tacit agreement, when either of them had been away. It had been some kind of universe thing, purely intuitive.

Passing familiar landmarks, Brad told himself he ought to turn around. The old days were gone. Things had ended badly between him and Meg anyhow, and she wasn't going to be at the Dixie Dog.

He kept driving.

He rounded a bend, and there was the Dixie Dog. Its big neon sign, a giant hot dog, was all lit up and going through its corny sequence—first it was covered in red squiggles of light, meant to suggest ketchup, and then yellow, for mustard.

Brad pulled into one of the slots next to a speaker, rolled down the truck window and ordered.

A girl roller-skated out with the order about five minutes later.

When she wheeled up to the driver's window, smiling, her eyes went wide with recognition, and she dropped the tray with a clatter.

Silently Brad swore. Damn if he hadn't forgotten he was a famous country singer.

The girl, a skinny thing wearing too much eye makeup, immediately started to cry. "I'm sorry!" she sobbed, squatting to gather up the mess.

"It's okay," Brad answered quietly, leaning to look down at her, catching a glimpse of her plastic name tag. "It's okay, Mandy. No harm done."

"I'll get you another dog and a shake right away, Mr. O'Ballivan!"

"Mandy?"

She stared up at him pitifully, sniffling. Thanks to the copious tears, most of the goop on her eyes had slid south. "Yes?"

"When you go back inside, could you not mention seeing me?"

"But you're Brad O'Ballivan!"

"Yeah," he answered, suppressing a sigh. "I know."

She rolled a little closer. "You wouldn't happen to have a picture you could autograph for me, would you?"

"Not with me," Brad answered.

"You could sign this napkin, though," Mandy said. "It's only got a little chocolate on the corner."

Brad took the paper napkin and her order pen, and scrawled his name. Handed both items back through the window.

She turned and whizzed back toward the side entrance to the Dixie Dog.

Brad waited, marveling that he hadn't considered incidents like this one before he'd decided to come back home. In retrospect, it seemed shortsighted, to say the least, but the truth was, he'd expected to be—Brad O'Ballivan.

Presently Mandy skated back out again, and this time she managed to hold on to the tray.

"I didn't tell a soul!" she whispered. "But Heather and Darlene *both* asked me why my mascara was all smeared." Efficiently she hooked the tray onto the bottom edge of the window.

Brad extended payment, but Mandy shook her head.

"The boss said it's on the house, since I dumped your first order on the ground."

He smiled. "Okay, then. Thanks."

Mandy retreated, and Brad was just reaching for the food when a bright red Blazer whipped into the space beside his. The driver's door sprang open, crashing into the metal speaker, and somebody got out in a hurry.

Something quickened inside Brad.

And in the next moment Meg McKettrick was standing practically on his running board, her blue eyes blazing.

Brad grinned. "I guess you're not over me after all," he said.

SPECIAL EDITION™

brings you a heartwarming
new McKettrick's story from

NEW YORK TIMES BESTSELLING AUTHOR

LINDA LAEL MILLER

THE MCKETTRICK
Way

Meg McKettrick is surprised to be reunited
with her high school flame, Brad O'Ballivan,
who has returned home to his family's
neighboring ranch. After seeing Meg again,
Brad realizes he still loves her. But the pride
of both manage to interfere with love...until
an unexpected matchmaker gets involved.

—— McKettrick Women ——

Available December wherever you buy books.

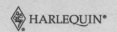

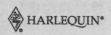

REQUEST YOUR FREE BOOKS!
2 FREE NOVELS PLUS 2 FREE GIFTS!

SPECIAL EDITION®
Life, Love and Family!

YES! Please send me 2 FREE Silhouette Special Edition® novels and my 2 FREE gifts. After receiving them, if I don't wish to receive any more books, I can return the shipping statement marked "cancel." If I don't cancel, I will receive 6 brand-new novels every month and be billed just $4.24 per book in the U.S., or $4.99 per book in Canada, plus 25¢ shipping and handling per book and applicable taxes, if any*. That's a savings of at least 15% off the cover price! I understand that accepting the 2 free books and gifts places me under no obligation to buy anything. I can always return a shipment and cancel at any time. Even if I never buy another book from Silhouette, the two free books and gifts are mine to keep forever.   235 SDN EEYU 335 SDN EEY6

Name	(PLEASE PRINT)

Address		Apt.

City	State/Prov.	Zip/Postal Code

Signature (if under 18, a parent or guardian must sign)

Mail to the **Silhouette Reader Service™**:
IN U.S.A.: P.O. Box 1867, Buffalo, NY 14240-1867
IN CANADA: P.O. Box 609, Fort Erie, Ontario L2A 5X3
Not valid to current Silhouette Special Edition subscribers.

Want to try two free books from another line?
Call 1-800-873-8635 or visit www.morefreebooks.com.

* Terms and prices subject to change without notice. NY residents add applicable sales tax. Canadian residents will be charged applicable provincial taxes and GST. This offer is limited to one order per household. All orders subject to approval. Credit or debit balances in a customer's account(s) may be offset by any other outstanding balance owed by or to the customer. Please allow 4 to 6 weeks for delivery.

Your Privacy: Silhouette is committed to protecting your privacy. Our Privacy Policy is available online at www.eHarlequin.com or upon request from the Reader Service. From time to time we make our lists of customers available to reputable firms who may have a product or service of interest to you. If you would prefer we not share your name and address, please check here. ☐

SSE07

Get ready to meet

THREE WISE WOMEN

with stories by

DONNA BIRDSELL, LISA CHILDS

and

SUSAN CROSBY.

Don't miss these three unforgettable stories
about modern-day women and the love
and new lives they find on Christmas.

Look for *Three Wise Women*
Available December wherever you buy books.

TheNextNovel.com

HN88147

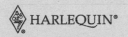

HARLEQUIN®

American ★ Romance®

Kate Merrill had grown up convinced
that the most attractive men were incapable
of ever settling down. Yet the harder she
resisted the superstar photographer
Tyler Nichols, the more persistent the
handsome world traveler became.
So by the time Christmas arrived, there
was only one wish on her holiday list—
that she was wrong!

LOOK FOR

THE CHRISTMAS DATE

BY

Michele Dunaway

Available December
wherever you buy books

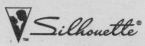

COMING NEXT MONTH

#1867 THE McKETTRICK WAY—Linda Lael Miller
Meg McKettrick longed for a baby—husband optional—and her rugged old flame, rodeo cowboy Brad O'Ballivan, was perfect father material. But Brad didn't want a single night of passion, he wanted love, marriage, the works. Now it was an epic battle of wills, as proud, stubborn Meg insisted on doing things her way...the McKettrick way.

#1868 A BRAVO CHRISTMAS REUNION—Christine Rimmer
Bravo Family Ties
Try as he might, coffeehouse-chain tycoon Marcus Reid couldn't get over his former executive assistant Hayley Bravo. But when Hayley had proposed to him seven months ago, he'd balked and she'd left town. Now a business trip reunited them...and clued Marcus in to the real reason for Hayley's proposal—he was about to be a daddy!

#1869 A COWBOY UNDER HER TREE—Allison Leigh
Montana Mavericks: Striking It Rich
Hotel heiress Melanie McFarlane took over Thunder Canyon Ranch to prove she could run a successful business on her own. But she needed help—bad—and enlisted local rancher Russ Chilton, telling his family he was her husband. Russ insisted on a legal marriage to seal the deal, and soon city slicker Melanie fell hard...for her husband.

#1870 THE MILLIONAIRE AND THE GLASS SLIPPER—Christine Flynn
The Hunt for Cinderella
When his tech mogul father delivered the ultimatum to marry and have kids within a year or be disinherited, family rebel J. T. Hunt decided to set up his own business before he was cut off. For help, he turned to a bubbly blond ad exec—but it was her subtly beautiful stepsister, Amy Kelton, who rode to the rescue as J.T.'s very own Cinderella.

#1871 HER CHRISTMAS SURPRISE—Kristin Hardy
Kelly Stafford thought she was engaged to the *good* Alexander sibling—until she walked in on him with another woman, and his money laundering threatened to land Kelly in jail! Now could his black-sheep brother, Lex Alexander—voted Most Likely To Get Arrested back in high school—save Kelly...and maybe even steal her heart in the process?

#1872 THE TYCOON MEETS HIS MATCH—Barbara Benedict
Sure it was surprising when writer Trae Andrelini's independent friend Lucy decided to marry stuffed-shirted mogul Rhys Paxton for security, and even more surprising when Lucy left him at the altar to go after an old boyfriend. But the biggest surprise of all? When free-spirited Trae discovered that Rhys was actually the man for *her*!

SSECNM1107